Close Combat

Also by James Albany in Pan Books

Warrior Caste
Mailed Fist
Deacon's Dagger

James Albany

Close Combat

Pan Original
Pan Books London and Sydney

First published 1983 by Pan Books Ltd,
Cavaye Place, London SW10 9PG

ISBN 0 330 28000 7

Photoset by Parker Typesetting Service, Leicester
Printed and bound in Great Britain by
Richard Clay (The Chaucer Press) Ltd, Bungay, Suffolk

Into the following account of actions conducted by certain officers and men of the Special Air Service squadrons during the State of Emergency in Malaya, I have taken the liberty of inserting direct quotations from letters written by Major Jeffrey Alexander Deacon MC to his former Commanding Officer, Colonel Peter Holms MBE, between November 1945 and the Colonel's death in 1957. I wish to express my gratitude to the Colonel's daughter, Mrs Judith Kempler of Catonsville, Maryland, for making the letters available; and to Captain Jeffrey Edward Deacon, presently serving with the 22nd Special Air Service Regiment, for permission to use extracts from his father's private and personal correspondence.

James Albany.

Above all else, and from the earliest moments of history, one primordial force has dominated the life of every man, woman and child in Malaya – the gentle Malays themselves, the industrious Chinese, the listless Indians, the perspiring British alike. It is the jungle; the jungle which none can escape, the jungle which reaches to the back of every compound, to the back of every mind; the jungle which blots out the sun over four fifths of Malaya's 50,850 square miles. Harsh and elemental, implacable to all who dare to trifle with its suffocating heat or hissing rains, the jungle alone has remained untamed and unchanged.

Noel Barber,
The War of the Running Dogs

Contents

1 The making of the enemy

Deacon to Holms: November 1945

It was obvious that day in your office that you were sick. Perhaps you are still sick for all I know. The truth is that I don't much care. I've used up all my pity. Not a drop remains. Not for you, not for the poor old pensioned-off SAS, not for myself. Especially not for myself.

When they eventually stitch me together and declare me fit for duty, I expect some cold-hearted bastard will endeavour to convince me that I should stay in the army. Perhaps the War Office will even offer me a comfortable billet as an officer/instructor with the TA. As far as I'm concerned they can stuff the TA. I owe no loyalty to you or to the regiment you helped create. I've certainly no intention of becoming a walking museum piece, showing off to silly young sods attracted by SAS glamour.

Glamour? My God! If I told them the truth about our shambles with the Russians at Baku-Ashran do you suppose they would find it glamorous? If I was indiscreet enough to mention that forty men accompanied you on that ill-advised raid on the airfield at El Harousse and only two returned alive, do you suppose the gilt might wear off the gingerbread? If I stripped and showed them what happened to me after I let you talk me into a solo mission as a so-called 'observer' do you suppose they would still flock to sign on the dotted line?

Yes, I know. It isn't your pigeon any more. It isn't your business, your concern. You no longer have the ear of the mysterious chums in Whitehall who asked you to find a fellow to drop into occupied Malaya and take a shuftie on their behalf. The fact that your chums in Whitehall were absolutely right to be apprehensive about Wei Sand Shan is no justification for what's happened. I don't mean to me, you understand. I mean to Shan.

A bloody MBE in the Victory Honours List. A bloody, bloody MBE. Who had that gem of an idea? Who rejected my report out of hand, discarded it as the ravings of a lunatic major who'd lost his nerve, his health and his sanity as a result of an unfortunate little escapade down in the jungles of the Peninsula? Which of your chums decided it wasn't 'politic' to expose the Chinese guerrillas for what they really are, ruthless bandits dedicated to the overthrow of democratic government and the instatement of communism as the dominant world power?

Chin Peng, Lau Yew, Sand Shan – they may have fought bravely by the side of the boys of Force 136 and be regarded by some as old comrades, but they gained more from the British than the British gained from them. Now that the Japanese are defeated, no matter what changes take place in Malaya, the British will become the enemy. Already *are* the enemy. Have *always* been the enemy. In six months or a year we'll be fighting the communists just as fiercely as ever we fought the Japanese or Germans. Believe me, I know. You sent me to snuffle for evidence of possible insurrection by the trained members of the Malayan Peoples' Anti-Japanese Army, and I found it. The evidence? I *am* the evidence, what's left of me.

Thunderheads of blue-black cloud were massed on the far horizon. The first pale flush of dawn smeared the rim of the Indian Ocean far to the north of Sumatra. It was as if the sun was coming up in the wrong quarter, like an omen. A brisk wind bowled the *kuehs* around the coast, straight towards the breakers which pounded the sand-bars at the mouth of the Imapoh river. We were drenched with spray and the muscular brown backs of the Malays who paddled and poled with expert ease were sleek with it. I was crouched among gear sacks wrapped in oilcloth to protect the weapons and explosives. I felt really charged as the fragile little boats lifted and swooped inshore. Dead ahead was the jungle, my first glimpse of it; forty shades of stygian darkness relieved only by the milky brown grin of the estuary of the Imapoh. I didn't know much about the operation but I had been told that I would be expected to swim the river belly down on an ocean board. To the boys of the Special Boat Section – Landsdown and Prince – it was fairly routine. I suspect they enjoyed it. But the prospect of a long swim up the dark infested river frightened me inordinately. You neglected to mention the river when you briefed me, by the way.

Rain had fallen on high ground in the region, and the river, I was told, would be thick with silt. We would be going in on the flood-tide, though, and it would give us headway against the current. I was assured by the SBS officers and by the New Zealand major, Hack Patterson, that a spot of the old cats-and-dogs was all to the good. Put the Nips off guard, give better cover, etc. I was not convinced.

It may have been my first foray in monsoon Asia but I had enough combat experience to realise that heavy rains meant the danger of delay to the Japanese freighter that was bringing the arms shipment into the port at Masang, or a hold-up of the convoy along the Masang highway, which isn't much more than a gravel track at the best of times. Snow, desert, jungle – timing's vital in small group raids and I was under the impression that Sand Shan would not be all that well organised.

Besides, the guerrilla groups had been pretty active along the west coast and Jap patrols would be at full strength. The arrival of a large shipment of brand-new weapons wasn't an event to be taken lightly. It was all going to hell and gone for the Japanese in South East Asia. Local commanders like Colonel Kajuto were feeling the pinch. Small wonder Kajuto was keen as mustard to put the shipment under lock and key. According to Patterson, Kajuto had been bred in the Samurai tradition and would fight to the last drop of blood rather than lose face. Swords aren't enough to put on an honourable show, though. For that you need all the modern weapons you can muster.

Before you dragged me away from the 1st SAS in Norway and the chore of disarming three hundred thousand Wehrmacht, I knew little of the war on the other side of the world. Your signal intrigued me. It also had that sinister ring which is your hallmark. I assumed that sitting behind a desk in London hadn't blunted your appetite for conspiracy. It was always a puzzle why you got the SAS – a more-or-less regular fighting unit– involved in cloak-and-dagger work. The war in Europe was virtually over, therefore I imagined you would be casting a covetous eye on the fighting in the Pacific and Far Eastern war zones; the SAS was a fighting regiment and would be put out of existence by a sudden outbreak of peace. When you informed me that I was off to Malaya to take part in a raid on a Jap convoy, however, I began to wonder if you had gone a little gaga. Even when you told me that you wanted me to 'assess' the strength of the guerrillas and their leader Sand Shan and that the raid would probably be the first of several such sorties, I still thought it was wasteful to transport a chap from the edge of the Arctic Circle to the Equator just for the exercise.

Incidentally, I wasn't deceived by your flattering comments about my adaptability. You knew I wouldn't baulk at the assignment. I never could resist a challenge, not even at the tail-end of five years of fighting. The fact that I couldn't tell a coconut tree from a mangrove didn't seem to matter. Patterson would be there to hold my hand. So, resigned if not absolutely brimful of joy, I zoomed out of West Horsfall in the RAF transport you'd laid on and winged my way to Gibraltar. Thence to Algiers and Cairo and on to Karachi, Bombay and Ceylon. It was a remarkably smooth trip, for once, with minimum delays. I began to feel more confident.

When I reached Colombo I was met by the pair of Special Boat Section wallahs who had been assigned to accompany me on the raid. Landsdown and Prince, hard, taciturn bastards, seemed to resent my instrusion on to their patch. It was as if they wanted to keep what was left of the war for themselves. I outranked them, of course, but I was at their mercy in that foreign environment.

Landsdown was in his early twenties but exuded a mature sort of arrogance. He was wedge-shaped, with sleek jet-black hair and eyes like a seal pup's.

His first question was tinged with sarcasm. 'You *do* swim, sir, don't you?'

Prince was a 1st Lieutenant too. He had crinkly brown hair and fine-boned features which made him appear delicate. If Landsdown was arrogant, Prince was plain sullen.

We didn't hang about in Colombo. We boarded the naval frigate *Seahound* directly. She steamed out of Colombo harbour into the Indian Ocean within a couple of hours of our arrival.

I was still under the impression that we would be dropped close to the Malayan shore by submarine. I expected the frigate to make contact with a sub and the three of us to be transferred to the submersible. Landsdown and Prince probably knew the truth but didn't bother to enlighten me. I received the distinct impression that the operation was fairly routine. They certainly weren't nervous about its outcome.

I asked Landsdown what he thought of Sand Shan.

'Bloody little banana-hat Chinkie peasant. Never be heard of again after Tojo surrenders,' was Landsdown's opinion.

I began to appreciate why you required an objective outside report and didn't trust the word of Special Force officers who worked in the region.

Major Hack Patterson was quite a different type. He was a most unlikely-looking commando, tall, skinny and balding. His legs were incredibly long and pale, all scarred and gashed. Three fingers on his left hand were missing. When I chinned him about the missing digits, all he said was, 'One should not forget where one sets one's own booby-traps, should one, old bean?' His voice was a dry whisper, legacy of some tropical illness. But he spoke rapidly and so cheerfully that I thought him a bit fey.

Since it was Patterson's show there was, of course, no submarine.

I was asleep in my bunk on board the frigate when Prince came to fetch me. I went up on deck with my dunnage, looking for the submarine. No sub. Patterson was standing in the prow of a sea-going junk hove to alongside the frigate. The setting sun was behind him, the two vessels heaving up and down though the sea seemed glassy calm. Prince, Landsdown and I, plus a fair quantity of equipment, transferred by dinghy to the junk and the *Seahound* steamed away.

Patterson greeted me like a long-lost brother. He escorted me to a cabin – a hut, really – pegged to the junk's aft-deck under the shelter of the gigantic mainsail. There, by the light of an oil lamp, he poured me a stiff whisky, spread out the maps and explained the plan.

Regular beach patrols made a standard surf landing risky. We would be dropped by fishing craft off the mouth of the Imapoh river and swim up it on ocean boards for a couple of miles. There we would make contact with Sand Shan on the river-bank in the jungle between the coastal posts and the Masang highway. The arms convoy was expected soon after dawn and Sand Shan would have his men in ambush positions. Prince and Landsdown would wait until the last truck had gone over the bridge which crossed the Imapoh and then blow it; a regular demolition job. Patterson and I would be with Shan along the highway to assist in destroying the trucks. I asked Patterson why Shan did not intend to remove the weapons from the convoy. Patterson's reply, in the light of what happened, was revealing.

'Not policy, old bean. The powers that be aren't too keen on weapons being salted away in the jungle.'

'What does Shan have to say to that edict?'

'No argument. He's well enough equipped. Besides he doesn't have the manpower to whisk a big load of arms to safety before the Japanese descend on us out of the garrison at Imapoh.'

'How far is the garrison from the attack point?'

'Five miles.'

'How many men will Shan have at his command?'

'Twenty. Thirty at most.'

There wasn't much else I needed to know.

Prince and Landsdown took me on deck, showed me an ocean board – ten feet long and shaped like an ironing-board – and told me how to ride it. After that, while the junk ploughed on, we ate a meal of cold fish and fruit and slept for an hour or two.

In the wee small hours, the junk made rendezvous with two inshore fishing vessels, *kuehs*, each with a crew of two Malays who had done this sort of thing for Patterson before. We were lowered into the little boats and set out for the distant coastline.

The glazed and shimmering surface which I had associated with the Indian Ocean was gone. Beery black waves climbed to crests bearded with foam. Fretful and strenuous, the head of the Strait of Malacca heaved between landmasses. The stink of the jungle reached out to me. It was heavy, fetid and cloying. It didn't smell like vegetation, like earth and the things which grew upon the earth. It smelled like an animal, a wet, shaggy beast. Carnivorous, of course.

The *kuehs* settled along the oily curve behind the breaker line. The Malays held them steady, dipping and twisting their paddles, aided by long rope-bound bamboo poles. Patterson told me that when he gave the word I was to take the ocean board and step over the side with it.

The *kuehs* swung abruptly, lifted and were driven by the breakers on to the shoal of sand and silt which lay just below the swirl. I could just see Prince and Landsdown swarming out of the lead boat into the surge. Ocean boards were slung on their shoulders and they carried oilcloth gear sacks in their arms. Because I was new at the game and a mere SAS lubber, my pack was light and pliant. When the Anzac touched my shoulder I slid the board upright and caught it by a webbing strap improvised from parachute harness. I drew it to my breast like a Saxon shield and stepped over the side of the boat, waist-deep into the sea.

Beneath my heels the sand sucked and dribbled. I wallowed forward quickly until I found the firm shoulder of the bar under my feet. I leaned against the sloping breakers and forgot to turn the board edge on as Landsdown had told me to do. I was almost bowled over backwards by the press of the waves. Naturally I didn't want to go arse over and appear like a complete idiot to the lieutenants from SBS, so I waded to the crown of the sand-bar in a hurry.

Patterson plunged by my side with a weird high step, like a flamingo on hot asphalt. We were clad in shorts and pullovers but it wasn't at all cold. Aerated, the water was like warm milk. Kneeling, I strapped the gear on to the board and lowered myself to it. The oilcloth roll, at chest level, made a comfortable pad. It helped raise my head so that I could see where I was going. Prince and Landsdown were already swimming across the stretch of water between the bar and the river mouth. I took a deep breath and thrust myself forward. Propelling the board with feet and hands, I swam into the deep water. Bolstered by the waves, the board scudded towards the shore. It was easy and I relaxed, rode without alarm into the brown estuary of the Imapoh.

The arms of the mangrove swamp and green jungle closed around me. Malaya itself seemed to swallow me up, though I was aware of Patterson behind me and, once we had left the sea behind, I could hear the soft splash of his limbs from time to time. Prince and Landsdown were lost in the darkness but I needed no guide. I kept paddling, not rushing it, about thirty yards out from the left shore of the river. Once the mouth of the Imapoh was past, the river broadened. Flood-tide or not, the downstream current was thrusting enough to tire one. After a couple of miles I found myself labouring a little. My back ached with the position on the board.

The blink of the torch on the bank was brief. But I was on the look-out for it and steered myself inshore. There was light in the sky, though the dense jungle blocked most of it. I caught a fleeting glimpse of Prince and Landsdown hauling themselves out of the water. We had made contact.

There was a boy on the tongue of dry, packed mud which was our landing site. He leaned forward and offered me his hand. I clasped it and he dragged me ashore. I rolled off the board, panting, while two men silently stole away my board and gear and vanished into the ferns with them. In the sodden pullover I was cold now. The boy touched my thigh. He handed me a half coconut shell. When I sniffed it I discovered it was rum. Holding the shell in both hands I drank gladly. The rum dribbled down my throat, warmed my innards and removed the soupy taste of the river.

'Sorry, no tea,' said the boy softly. 'No muffins.'

He seemed pleased to see me, though his smile was shy. He wore a flak-jacket and a floppy hat with the brim turned down. His features were smooth, almost unformed, and his neck was as slender as a wand.

Revived, I returned the shell and tapped the boy on the knee by way of thanks.

'Now, you come with me,' he whispered.

I was sopping wet and the dawn air was cold but I assumed there would be an assembly before the attack and hoped that I would have a chance to change then.

The jungle was much more dense that I had anticipated. Palms, ferns, thorns were all stitched together with creepers, dripping with the aftermath of the rain squall. Unencumbered I followed closely on the boy's heels as he slid into head-high undergrowth. The path was vague and narrow. It was still, unnervingly still. There were no audible night-sounds. Everything seemed muffled. Sense told me that there would be no dangerous animals in the vicinity and there probably wasn't a snake within miles. The activity of the guerrillas would have scared them all off. I was not afraid, not even of the Japanese. Bent low, I padded after my guide for about a quarter of a mile. The path petered out in a small shrouded clearing at the foot of a cluster of distinctive grey-boled trees. A dozen or so men were gathered there including Landsdown, Prince and Hack Patterson.

Dressed in combat rig, the SBS men were stowing charges into rucksacks. In a sleeveless jerkin and shorts, Patterson was seated on the ground clipping grenades to a webbing belt. If this was Wei Sand Shan's entire outfit, it was very small indeed. The guerrillas appeared well trained, however. Not a light showed. They made hardly a sound. They were armed with carbines and Stens and sat casually on their haunches awaiting the signal to set off for the highway. I hadn't a clue how far we were from the highway. I was disoriented after the swim. My watch indicated that it was five minutes past six o'clock, but time meant nothing in practical terms. I had to be content to be a passenger on the raid.

Patterson beckoned me to him. He whispered, 'See you've met Sand Shan.'

'Have I?'

The boy was by our side, having followed me without invitation.

He said, 'I am Sand Shan, sir.'

He reached for my hand and gave it a tug.

'I'm Deacon. Special Air Service.'

'Very fine outfit. Very courageous.'

I thanked him.

'Have you fought in my country before?' he asked.

'No, the desert was my stamping ground.'

'Ah, yes. Were you with Major Stirling?'

'Holms was my CO.'

'I have not heard of Holms.'

'He's heard of you,' I said. 'He speaks highly of your exploits, Sand Shan.'

'How complimentary.'

The guerrilla leader was excessively polite in the manner of an upper-form schoolboy. He spoke perfect English with just a trace of a 'Burlington Bertie' accent. I suspect he was educated at one of the Singapore colleges, possible Gladstone – though you probably had his term reports in your desk all along.

Mindful of my mission, I asked Shan if this was his total force.

'There are a few more chaps. In position by the highway.'

'How many, in total?'

He evaded my question. 'Will you accompany me, please, Major Deacon?'

I asked about my gear bag and it was brought to me. I was slightly pipped to discover it had been opened. But I said nothing. I stripped off my wet pullover and shorts and put on combat trousers, bush jacket and calf-length, rubberised boots. I buckled on a webbing belt, checked my revolver and holstered it. I even put on the old regimental beret. I was, after all, going into action. For once I must have looked awfully neat and respectable, quite a model little commando in fact.

Hack Patterson patted me on the shoulder. 'Chin up, old bean. It'll be a cake-walk, you'll see.'

Light was held in a seeping mist. The jungle was devoid of sounds, except for the faint, half-hearted drone of insects. Walking erect, Sand Shan led the column out of the little clearing on to a prepared track through the undergrowth. Prince and Landsdown had gone off without a word of farewell, accompanied by four of the guerrillas. I hadn't had a chance to wish them luck.

I walked directly behind Wei Sand Shan, Patterson behind me. I noticed that Shan carried a big old-style Colt .38 semi-automatic which he wore slung from a chest holster. Burdened with weapons, the rest of the People's Army slithered like a long snake at our heels.

I felt awkward in the jungle, with fronds and grasses clinging to me in that narrow, narrow tunnel. Patterson travelled well, in spite of his height and angularity. He had a comical crouched gait, like the Marx brother with the moustache and cigar. I was prepared for a lengthy hike. I was surprised, therefore, when Shan stopped and held up his hand, indicating that we had almost reached the highway. I couldn't see a damned thing except foliage. It still seemed like the middle of the night though it was, in fact, full daylight by now.

Exceptionally well disciplined, the guerrillas broke from the path in ones and twos and vanished into the undergrowth.

I touched Patterson's arm, made the hand-sign for 'bridge'. Patterson jerked his thumb to the right. There was still no sound to tell me that a highway lay ahead, a highway protected by several hundred Japanese soldiers.

I distinctly remember how Wei Sand Shan unbuttoned his fly and, kneeling on the ground, pissed; how Patterson closed his eyes for a moment and touched his maimed hand to a religious medallion which hung about his neck on a silver chain. His lips moved. Perhaps it was a prayer for deliverance, or an ancient Maori war-chant. As usual I slipped out my revolver and checked its working parts to make sure that the muzzle hadn't dropped off or the bullets fallen out.

Sand Shan cupped his hand over my ear.

'It is necessary to cross the highway. Keep very close to me, please,' he hissed.

I nodded.

On hands and knees Shan crawled into the lush grasses which flourished beneath the hardy plants.

I followed.

The ground was soft as latex. It rose on to a ramp of reddish earth mixed with sand and gravel. Shan flattened himself against the ramp. I did likewise. Patterson was beside me on my right. The highway was four or five feet above our heads. It was in an excellent state of repair by the look of it. Broader than I had thought it would be, though hardly Watling Street. The growl of an engine caused me to duck. Nose pressed into my hands, I didn't see what manner of machine shot past. It sounded powerful, no tin Lizzie. It boomed away rapidly, leaving silence in its wake.

Shan crawled forward once more, Patterson and I close beside him. Exhaust fumes were sharp in the fetid heat. The road was deserted. We went across it like lizards, scuttling into straw-like clumps of grass on the far side.

Hardly had we got there when a strange procession came into view along the highway – four motor-cyclists, with armed passengers in side-cars. The motorised bicycles were three-wheelers, similar to the trishaws you see in Singapore. They had thin rubber tyres and were powered by 250cc engines. The side-cars were made of wickerwork, like bath chairs. Here in the middle of the jungle the things looked ridiculously jaunty. A command car followed the bikes, an ordinary sort of vehicle with a dismembered soft top. It was piled with soldiers, a swaying pyramid, carbines sticking out. My first glimpse of Jap fighting men. They did not seen particularly barbarous. Unprepossessing and doleful, they clung like gibbons to the frame of the fast-moving car. The driver of the motor-car wore goggles which covered most of his face.

The car passed, braked and, about three hundred yards north of our position, halted. Four infantrymen jumped down and made a search of the surrounding bush. They moved with jerky little steps and much stabbing of carbines. Sweating, I watched them through the leaves of grass. The command car rolled on again, leaving the four soldiers on the highway. They relaxed when the car was out of sight and strolled away from us towards Imapoh village.

The country was alien, the enemy a different colour, but I had been in ambush situations too often to be really nervous.

After three or four minutes I heard the rumble of trucks on the span of the bridge.

I unbuttoned my holster and slid the butt of the revolver into my palm. I had brought a Sten with me but God knows where it had gone to. I suppose Shan gave it to one of his henchmen in case I got too free with it. Who knows? Patterson was tense, vulpine features drawn in a rictus of nervous anticipation. He had tucked the religious medallion beneath his shirt to stop it winking in the sunlight. But there was no sunlight, only a humid, muggy, lime-tinted haze.

The crash of the trucks grew louder. Crumbs of gravel dribbled from the road shoulder. Parting the grass, I stared along the highway. Two more of the odd little motor-cycles preceded the column of the trucks. Patterson told me they were products of the Mitsubishi works but to me they looked like Leyland three-tonners decorated with Jap script and insignia. Canvas tops were furled. There was a complement of guards with each truck. The convoy was clipping along at about fifteen mph but there was remarkably little dust.

So far I'd seen little of Wei Sand Shan's army. I began to wonder if we were expected to tackle the convoy by ourselves. Motor-cycles prowled past us, then the first of the trucks. I resisted the temptation to raise my head. I watched wheels rumble only a dozen feet from me. I took out my revolver. At any moment the last of the trucks would clear the Imapoh bridge, Landsdown and Prince would blow it sky-high and all hell would break loose.

The initial explosion was an anti-climax, muffled and faint, like a hippo breaking wind under water. But the second explosion was beautiful.

A deep, ripping volley of sound tore along the road and made the trees bow before it. Above the jungle tops I saw black smoke. And then I was on my feet. Up ahead the road had been blocked by more detonations, a couple of huge palm trees blown across it to close off the section. I remember thinking how much the chaps of my unit of the SAS would have enjoyed the situation. We would have done a wonderful job on those trucks long before Kajuto's officers mustered a rescue mission and dragged it out of the garrison. All it would have taken would have been a dozen lads of the calibre of Campbell and McNair. But Sand Shan did not intend to destroy the transports. Sand Shan had lied all along the line, lied about the size of his army, lied about his need for Allied assistance.

Japanese infantry. Circular steel helmets, tape leggings,

cross-band ammo pouches. Nagoya submachine-guns, M.38s. Grenades. Mounted machine-guns? None that I could see. Jap guards were hitting the dirt. They sprang off the trucks with the agility of sand fleas. It wasn't cowardice but bitter experience which made them abandon the vehicles without a fight. The Japanese could see at a glance that they were heavily outnumbered.

I'd been told that there were thirty thousand trained guerrilla troops in South East Asia, It seemed as if Shan had mustered most of them for the arms raid at Imapoh. There were Chinese everywhere. All armed. All firing. Battle cries, screams, the manic chatter of the submachine-guns, the whanging of rifle bullets in the narrow slot of the highway. Men and more men. The Japs hadn't a chance.

Bullets raked them, a mighty concentration of small-arms fire. But it wasn't backed with grenades or mortar shelling. Nothing damaged the crates roped in the rear of the trucks. Sprawled grotesquely by the wheels of the trucks lay Japanese dead and dying. Some flopped on the verge or lay, as if devoured, with feet and legs sticking out of the undergrowth.

I did nothing. I didn't dare step on to the road, into the vee-concentration of fire. The road was a slaughterhouse. The attack was over within minutes of the explosions. I didn't even send off a single shot. My contribution was nil. My presence was utterly superfluous. Shan needed no assistance. He had an army of three hundred or more at his command.

Why did Shan ask Patterson to enlist SBS aid? To blow the bridge? Possibly. But he could probably have managed that without Prince and Landsdown. Suddenly I was apprehensive. Whatever rumours had wafted back to London had substance. Wei Sand Shan *was* strong, very strong. The setting-up of the arms raid suggested an organisation far superior to that which you believed existed. Whitehall would be most interested in what I had seen.

I stepped out on to the road. Two Japanese soldiers lay dead at my feet. Their round helmets did not tip off. Long cotton tapes were elaborately and securely knotted around their jaws. Blood stained the backs of their tunics like sweat. I looked away from the corpses. I expected to see fighting, some token resistance from the Nips. But it was all over. Shan's army was in complete command.

Already they were hauling the crates from the backs of the trucks.

Patterson stood by my side. 'Mother of God! Where did they spring from?'

'Suppose you tell me.'

'I had no idea, no idea there were so many.'

'Well? Do we fire the trucks?' I inquired.

'I wouldn't if I were you. Wouldn't dare lay a finger on them.'

Obviously Patterson had been kept in the dark about Shan's intentions.

'Why didn't he tell us?' I said.

Patterson fingered the medallion at his throat.

'Must have been heap big pow-wow. Top secret,' said Patterson. 'Shan's been rather out of it lately. He has it in for some of the executives in the Communist Party. Believes that Communist number one, chap called Lai Tek, sold the CP to the Japanese.'

It was a bizarre package course in contemporary affairs, standing there with Chinese guerrillas swarming all around and dozens of Niponese corpses strewn at my feet.

'What does that have to do with us?' I said.

Patterson sighed loudly. 'It may be that Shan thinks we – British Intelligence – put Lai Tek up to it.'

'Did we?'

'What? No, no. Of course not, old bean.'

'Listen,' I said. 'Did Wei Sand Shan *ask* for Allied help on this one?'

'He . . . he asked me to come along, yes.'

'And SBS and SAS involvment?'

'That,' Patterson admitted, 'was my idea.'

'In God's name, why?'

'For protection, I suppose.'

'What's Shan up to?'

'Oh, he makes no bones about the fact that he wants no truck with the British after the Japanese are expelled from Malaya. He has one objective, to stick a Communist government in power.'

'Backed by the Russians?'

'Probably,' said Patterson.

'And Shan's bosses, the official CP wallahs?'

'They believe it should not be done precipitately. All for talkee-talkee. Councils and committees, sort of thing.'

'And Shan?'

'I have the feeling all he wants is bloodshed.'

Random shots drifted down the line of the convoy. The guerrillas took no prisoners. The wounded were being summarily dispatched. It isn't the style of the SAS, I admit, but in the Far East it's the rule of tit for tat; the Japanese started it. Shan was supervising the unloading of the arms crates. He was not easily distinguishable in the flock of guerrillas. He didn't radiate charisma. He looked, I thought, like a little drummer-boy in one of those sentimental Victorian battle paintings, lost, bewildered and innocent.

Patterson was shaken by what had occurred. He fumbled a tobacco tin from his jacket pocket and extracted two cigarettes, handed one to me. I put it in my mouth. The paper turned soggy as it absorbed sweat from my lips.

Patterson struck a match.

Wei Sand Shan was beside us instantly. Angrily he dashed the match from Patterson's hand.

'No smoking, please.'

'Sorry,' said Patterson, abashed.

'We are perforating the petrol tanks. It would be unfortunate if you started the fires before we are ready.'

'I thought that's why we were on this ride, Shan,' I said. 'To start fires.'

'Ah, but the attack was so very successful,' Shan smiled. 'It seems rather a pity to waste such a large collection of weapons.'

'But you don't need them,' I said. 'Do you?'

'Not yet,' said Wei Sand Shan. 'Come, gentlemen, we will take ourselves away from here before the Japanese arrive in force.'

'Where are my comrades?' I demanded. 'Lieutenants Prince and Landsdown.'

'They will join us later.'

'Where?'

'At a rendezvous. They will be guided to the place.'

'According to my schedule,' said Patterson, 'we're supposed to head for the coast.'

'Quite impossible,' said Sand Shan. 'Japanese patrol boats are off the river mouth.'

It was on the tip of my tongue to ask him how he got his information but he would have fobbed me off with a casual reply.

It had all been a damned waste, like a training exercise not a real raid at all. I glanced across the highway to the impenetrable wall of jungle. I had a mad impulse to make a break for it right there and then. The coast could not be more than four miles away. Surely, even a novice could find his way to the sea.

'Where exactly are you taking us, Shan?' said Patterson.

'To a place near the Takua.'

'The caves?'

'Close to the caves.'

'I thought the location of the Takua caves was secret?' Patterson said.

'It is,' said Shan. 'But we are allies, Major. We trust each other with secrets, do we not? Come along, gentlemen.'

The crates of weapons and ammo had been stripped out of the trucks. I'd never seen a job done faster or more efficiently. All the porters had been swallowed up by the jungle and only a dozen or so uniformed guerrillas remained in sight, darting down the line of trucks. I saw the flare of oil torches, pale in the daylight, and heard the cries of the Chinese as they kept in communication. The reek of petrol came down the highway very strongly. Then there was the soft thud of inflammable liquid igniting and blue fire slithered on the gravel.

Sand Shan caught my arm. 'Time to go, Major Deacon.'

End-of-line trucks were blazing now and, an instant later, one of them exploded as its tank expanded in the fierce heat. Grenades, like coconuts, dropped out of the jungle and caused the road surface to erupt in several places. If the Japanese at the garrison had not heard the earlier ruckus they could hardly fail to catch the sounds of this one.

'Thanks, but we'll find our own way home,' said Patterson.

Wei Sand Shan would have none of it. An entourage of six armed guerrillas appeared at the edge of the jungle. We didn't have the stomach for argument. Besides Landsdown and Prince were out there somewhere and it wouldn't do to abandon them to Shan's tender mercy.

Reluctantly Hack Patterson and I allowed ourselves to be led deeper into the hinterland, into Shan's domain.

I couldn't – and still can't – understand why Shan bothered to drag us all the way back to the Takua. There must have been an element of malice in it. I wasn't fooled now by his shy good manners or his smile. Wei Sand Shan was an Oriental tainted by the doctrines of Russia. The personality that had emerged from this mix, like a new strain of germ, was too much for a simple commando like Patterson to understand. What Shan planned wasn't 'cricket'. It certainly wasn't 'policy'. I doubt if the Malayan CP bigwigs would have condoned such directness. The long hike stuck in my craw more than anything. It made what happened seem cold-blooded and calculated. The trek wasn't necessary to escape the Japanese and, all along, without quite believing it, I had the feeling that Shan was taking us to a strange hidden place to do us in.

Sapped by the humidity, I found it difficult to remain alert. I couldn't begin to estimate how far the Takua was from the highway, and the highway from the coast. Miles have a different value in that sort of country.

We were preceded by three Malays in loincloths who broke trail. I don't mean that they had to hack through the undergrowth. There was a track of sorts and the natives kept to it, navigators in the great seething green sea of trees and shrubs. There were more guerrillas at the rear of the file to ensure we didn't leave tell-tales for the Japanese to pick up. We were strung out for most of the hike. I reckon distance covered couldn't have been more than a couple of miles in the hour which, for Malaya, is pretty damned quick.

Mid-morning saw a slight change in the monotonous jungle. I had the impression that the trail was rising, undergrowth thinning. We began to run across rocks clustered in the lushness. The pace of the hike quickened. Like a Boy Scout patrol leader, Sand Shan legged it out manfully. We saw nobody else, not a soul. Considering the number of porters who had vanished into the jungle and were, presumably, heading for the same spot as we were, that was quite a phenomenon. I had the feeling that it was towards a ridge that the trail climbed. I wasn't unduly surprised when the track emerged from the trees on to a scrumble of rock below a low, tusk-yellow escarpment.

It was hardly a ridge. Even here the jungle had only slackened its grip slightly and surrounding boulders looked as if they had been dipped in green treacle. Nonetheless it was a relief to reach the point of rendezvous, to glimpse blue sky and feel the faint waft of a breeze on one's brow.

The path writhed along the base of a forty-foot-high rock face. Though buried in the heart of the jungle, the knob of the summit of this formation gave excellent view-lines in all directions. There were caves in the vicinity too and, all in all, it was a perfect site for a secret camp.

'Nice little fort, isn't it, old bean?' said Patterson.

The Anzac seemed to have left his apprehension behind. He surveyed the scene cheerfully and with interest.

'Wouldn't General Kajuto love to know its bearings?' Patterson said.

'It would profit the Japanese nothing,' said Shan. 'By tomorrow we will all be gone and no trace will be left here.'

'How long have you been here?' I asked.

'Three weeks. It was our meeting-place for the organisation of the raid.'

'It's not your permanent base, then?'

'We have no permanent base.'

I wiped my face with a sodden handkerchief. 'Shan, why *have* you brought us here?'

'Good question,' said Patterson. 'I'm supposed to return these gentlemen safe and sound to the contact at Ophon. And that's miles away.'

Sand Shan shrugged. 'It is too dangerous to go to Ophon.'

'You knew the plan. You didn't say anything then. Why has it suddenly become dangerous?'

'Japanese patrols.'

'Blithering nonsense. We're slippery fellows.'

'Do you have a contact in Ophon too?' said Shan.

I realised that Patterson was about to blurt out the name of an Allied agent in this place. Quickly I intervened. 'How far is Ophon from here?'

'Too far for tonight's date with destiny,' said Patterson.

'Perhaps Mr Shan has another means of getting us out of Malaya?' I suggested.

'It will be safe here for a while,' said Shan, evading my question again. 'There is food and fresh water.'

'Hold on,' said Patterson. 'While we're at it, why didn't you tell me you intended to steal the arms shipment?'

'Impulse,' said Shan. 'It went so well I changed my mind.'

'Impulse be damned. You lied to me, Shan.'

'We will eat now and talk later.'

'I want an explanation, Shan.'

'Later, Major Patterson.'

Having no choice we followed the guerrilla along the path towards a rank of tall palms beneath which were half a dozen awnings and tents and a cooking pit with pots simmering over wood. Fresh water in jerrycans was stored under one of the awnings. On the ground were bed-rolls and rucksacks. There were only a dozen or so guerrillas, though. Most of them appeared to be convalescing from wounds.

It was cool under the trees which caught the breeze that dithered down from the ridge.

'Where exactly are these mysterious caves?' asked Patterson peevishly.

'The entrance is well hidden,' Shan answered.

I squinted up at the rock. There must have been sentries up

there, observers, but I couldn't see hilt nor hair of them. Shan was a clever little devil and had trained his fighters well. There was probably the basis of an arsenal here already and the big theft of Jap arms would add to it.

'Rest,' said Shan. 'Eat and rest.'

A Malay scooped stew from one of the pots and brought it to us in a mess-tin. He served Shan first then Patterson and me. We seated ourselves at the base of one of the trees. The bark was smooth and silvery. I removed my belt, beret, boots and socks. I was almost too tired to be hungry. I ate the food. It was hot and spicy and had lumps of real meat in it. I drank water from an aluminium pan which the native brought round.

It was hard to believe that the Peninsula belonged to the Japanese and not to Shan's guerrillas. As I ate I studied the walls of the jungle. It was no small wonder that so many special units, like Force 136, had been able to survive, even to flourish, in this country. Apart from the coastal strips it was no place for man to live. But here we were, comfortable and secure not more than a dozen miles from a Jap garrison.

I finished the stew, drank more water, leaned my shoulders against the tree bole. My eyelids were heavy, my limbs relaxed. Cool shade. Cool leaves stirring in the cool, cool breeze.

I fell asleep.

I have no idea how long I slept, about three hours I imagine. When I wakened I felt languorous and well rested. The light had grown sombre again, jade-green. The shadows of the palms were long. Patterson was stooping over me and it was his whisper which had wakened me.

'Deacon. Deacon.'

Beyond the Anzac I could see the corner of the track. Prince and Landsdown, in a lather of sweat and frustration, were toiling along it accompanied by a file of porters bringing in the first of the arms crates. Eight or nine banded crates were piled close to the water cans. A pair of gnarled, coffee-skinned natives were prising out the nails that banded the crates, supervised by one of Shan's officers.

Prince was mad as the devil. He caught sight of us and stumped over. His tunic was black with sweat and his curly hair was pasted down.

'What the hell is this? Where the bloody hell are we?'

'Keep your shirt on, old bean,' said Patterson.

'Aren't we supposed to ship out tonight?' Prince raged. 'In, hit, out. Trekking wasn't on the bloody programme.'

'Apparently there's been a change in plan.'

'Whose idea was it?' said Landsdown.

'Shan's, as a matter of fact.'

'Bloody Chinks. Can't trust them to do anything right.'

'Trouble at Ophon?' said Landsdown.

'Not too sure,' said Patterson evasively.

'Well, at least they've laid on supper,' said Prince and, still grumbling, headed for the cooking pots.

Landsdown was less easily appeased. 'Listen, did you know the guerrillas didn't blast the trucks after all? Pinched the whole damned cargo. There are hundreds of the little bastards hauling the stuff through the jungle right now.'

'Yes. We know,' said Patterson.

'What are they up to?'

'Not sure. Best shut up and sit tight for a bit.'

Suspiciously Landsdown shifted his gaze to me. 'Have you anything to do with all this, Major?'

'What do you mean?'

'Is this some SAS stunt in the making?'

'Don't be absurd.'

Unconvinced, Landsdown was drawn away from further conversation by his appetite. Together the SBS men carried their food to the base of another palm tree and huddled there, eating ravenously, muttering to each other.

Shan returned from the mouth of the track. Crates were arriving thick and fast now. I had a vision of dozens of invisible trails through the tropical forest converging on that one path. I could imagine ant-like columns toting crates determinedly. It became clear why all the guerrillas were Chinese. On principle no Malay would put himself through that much labour.

'Did you sleep well, Major Deacon?' Shan said.

I got to my feet. 'Any sign of the Japs?'

'A trifling attempt at pursuit – which was prevented.'

'We'll be on our way at first light,' said Patterson.

'Kajuto will be combing the area tomorrow. He is acquainted with my methods, however.' Wei Sand Shan laughed. 'The Japanese call me "The Invisible Warrior". It is rather flattering, what?'

'Kajuto will be going through the villages like a dose of salts. Retribution,' said Patterson.

'It is the Japanese way. It is not our way. When this war ends we will be remembered as friends of the poor people of Malaya. It will seem that we delivered them from the heel of the oppressor.'

'Meaning,' I said, 'the Japanese.'

'In the beginning,' said Sand Shan.

'And in the end?' I said.

Shan said, 'In the end – who knows?'

'You have an army, and weapons . . .'

'Do you know, Major, the British will expect us to hand over our weapons meekly when the war is won? We will be told to surrender every rifle, every shell. Perhaps we will be given a parade, a medal or two, and a handful of pennies. But then the imperialists will return, and their servile agents will rule the people once more.'

'Who exactly are you fighting for, Shan?' I said.

'For the poor and the oppressed.'

'For Malaya?' I said. 'Or for Russia?'

Shan's smile became fixed. He did not look at me but stared at a point past my right shoulder. 'There is enough light. We will go to the caves now.'

'Why?' I said.

'You must see the caves.'

'I'm not much of a one for visiting caves,' I said. 'I think I'll just stay put.'

'You will come.'

'Hold on, Shan. This is a British officer, I'll have you know,' said Patterson. 'You're not talking to some rubbed-out Indian servant.'

Shan raised his right hand, forefinger erect. The gesture reminded me of that made by a cricket umpire when a wicket falls. It was obviously a prearranged signal. Four guerrillas were by Shan's side on the instant. The clack of bolt-action carbines was loud in the clearing. Activity halted along the path and by the cooking pit. Men whom I had supposed asleep were suddenly wide awake. We had provoked the little bastard too far and too soon. I had no chance to go for my gun which was over by the tree bole along with my tunic and boots.

Bewildered and still buzzing with annoyance, Prince and Landsdown got to their feet, mess-tins in their hands.

'To the caves,' said Shan, very softly.

'So you may shoot us in private, Shan?' I said.

In a bantering tone Patterson protested. 'Come on now, Shan, old bean. We've had our differences of opinion before. Shouldn't talk politics, should we? Not good for the old *esprit de corps*. Mother of God, man, we're friends.'

'You are not my friend, Major Patterson.'

'All right. Ally then.'

'You are a spy, Major Patterson.'

''Course I'm a bloody spy.'

'No, I do not mean against the Japanese.I think you are a spy against me, against my people.'

'Don't be bloody ridiculous.'

'Did you not work with Lai Tek?'

'Well, yes. For six months or so, in the early days.'

'Did you not assist, Major Patterson, when Lai Tek sold out the Malayan Communist Party to the Japanese?'

'I don't know what you're—'

'Was it not at the instigation of the British that you told Lai Tek to reveal our meeting-place and allowed the Japanese to assassinate fifty-six of our ranking officers?'

Patterson spun towards me with an expression of helpless appeal. 'Deacon, for heaven's sake, what's he talking about?'

I was only too familiar with the deviousness of British Special Operations Executives. I could not be at all sure that Patterson *was* innocent. Perhaps Wei Sand Shan had justice on his side. He was certainly shrewd enough to deduce the truth, whereas the other Communist leaders were blinded by the need for cooperation.

Sand Shan went on, 'Is it not true, Major Patterson, that you were Lai Tek's contact with Special Forces HQ?'

'Christ, boy! I'm *your* contact with HQ.'

I said, 'Shan, if you have it in for Patterson why did you invite three strangers to join in this raid?'

Shan shook his head. 'I did not invite you, Major Deacon. It was Major Patterson's idea.'

'We just happened to be in the wrong place at the wrong time,' I said. 'That doesn't make us your enemy.'

'Britisher,' said Sand Shan, 'you *are* my enemy.'

I'm convinced that Prince had no notion of what was going on. Perhaps it was Shan's withering tone or the derisory manner in which he pronounced the word 'Britisher'. For whatever reason Prince took umbrage and flew into a paroxysm of rage.

'You traitorous fucking Chink!' Prince shouted. *'Who do you think you are to accuse—'*

The SBS officer flung his meal-tin at Shan. The guerrilla ducked but collected a splatter of stew gravy across his chest.

'Prince, wait!' I cried.

It was too late.

Prince hurled himself like a panther at Wei Sand Shan.

He was only ten or fifteen paces from the Communist when he made his move but covered no more than three before a fusillade from the carbines mowed him down. His jaw sagged, his eyes flared. He crumpled in mid-air, knees jack-knifing into his belly, and crouched on the beaten earth like a praying Mohammedan.

Wei Sand Shan shot him with the Colt revolver through the back of the head.

Landsdown was gunned down where he stood, shot several times in the back.

I didn't wait for my turn.

Twisting I chopped the nearest guerrilla on the throat and trampled over him. A first volley plucked at the leaves around me as I hurled myself into the foliage as into water. Neck-rolling I dived through slashing thorns and plunged down a slope coated with greasy clover-like plants. I was only yards from the edge of the encampment when a bullet thumped into my side. I pitched forward with the shock of the wound and rolled again, tumbling, wondering if I was dead.

In undergrowth I got up on one knee. I could see the blood patch and ripped at my shirt and swabbed with it – all this in a pause that lasted no longer than a couple of seconds – and saw to my relief that I had only been gouged along the waist girdle, a flesh-wound. By the feel of it no bones had been smashed though the wound stung like the devil. I clamped the wad of shirting to it and dived down the slope again chased by another volley from the hill above.

Desperation drove me on. I had no choice of direction, no difficult decisions to make. No basis upon which to make judgements of any kind. In those first few frantic minutes I discarded reason in favour of speed.

As luck would have it I had struck out from the clearing at its northern corner. Here the escarpment wrinkled into a catchment and a stream had carved a natural track through the enshrouding undergrowth. From the high ground of the Takua the stream hopped down a boulder bed for a quarter of a mile before dribbling into the listless jungle.

Instinctively I followed the stream.

I bounded down the boulder bed. Spears of shadow spiked the route. I ran as tightly as possible, trying to control my panic, to keep balance. My naked feet hurt worse than the bullet wound and I kept my teeth clenched and my head low. The trees protected me. Benevolent jungle cover. Rifle shots and Sten fire whizzed overhead. I realised that I had a very thin edge on the guerrillas. I ran with total concentration.

The descending sun and the erratic path of the stream gave me pointers. I was heading for the coast. The coast was my only possible avenue of escape. Between me and the ocean lay fifteen or twenty miles of hostile jungle. Plus Japs, aboriginal natives, crocodiles, poisonous snakes, and God knew what else. Behind me the guerrillas were in hot pursuit. I had absolutely nothing. No map, compass or water-bottle. No boots. No gun.

In the best tradition of the good old SAS, though, I tried to stifle negative thoughts – and keep right on going.

You may be wondering what all the fuss was about. Twenty miles and a head start? No problem. True, in the desert it would have been easy to navigate and a mere twenty miles constituted a stroll before lunch. But you have no notion of what the jungle is like until you've experienced it for yourself. Besides I was a total stranger to Malaya. I hadn't even had an opportunity to bone up on the damned country, to memorise its basic geography.

I had a hazy recollection of reading somewhere that Malayan jungle is the most impenetrable in the world. Also that its rivers are infested with crocodiles and that the buffalo is more ferocious than the tiger. But such creatures could hardly have been more deadly than the pack on my tail.

I did not dare be caught. I must push myself to the ultimate and forge on until dark. Survival was uppermost in my mind. I was also filled with loathing for Wei Sand Shan's method of justice and fired by determination to find my way back to an Allied base and see to it that he was punished for his crime. Shooting British officers would not exactly endear Shan to officials in the People's Army. It would most certainly awaken policy-makers in London to the inherent risks involved in trusting Communist guerrillas one inch.

The stream broadened. Its water changed from the colour of gin to *café au lait* as its course became deeper. Soon it was no longer a stream but a river and had a sluggish current to move it along.

I kept to the left bank, wading in shallows under huge trees. The water was thigh-deep. Now and then I would slither into a pot-hole or trough and, gasping with the effort and the pain of the gash in my side, would wade chest deep for three or four yards until I managed to drag myself out again.

The shape of the river was written above, pinkish sky stencilled out of the massive green growth. I followed it like a pilgrim. I had had food and some sleep and I was fit enough. Even so forty minutes out from Takua I began to labour. Heat and humidity and loss of blood sapped me. I fought an urge to flop on a mud bank or crawl into the fronds and lie there, let the ants or mosquitoes devour me. Naturally I didn't succumb to the temptation, being mindful of the fact that Shan's men were probably hot on my trail or had even got ahead of me.

Again the character of the river changed. Stones choked the channel. A huge brown pool swooped away to my right. It supported a floating raft of vegetation which may or may not have been an island. I ignored the pool and clambered over the stones, putting up a flock of big black-and-white birds which had been feeding along the shallows. The birds rose with a gabble that you might have heard in Singapore.

I waded out into the river once more.

It occurred to me that perhaps I should abandon the river entirely. But I was terrified of becoming lost in the jungle. Even if the river was the most obvious out-route, it was the best, the only choice for me. I was still fairly confident that I could outstrip the guerrillas by stamina and perseverance. When it grew dark, though, I would have to lie up.

How much ground had I actually covered? Five miles? Seven? It felt like fifty. I craved rest. But I had been in enough scrapes to know that in certain situations the most dangerous thing one can do is to stop moving.

I was bleeding badly from the flesh-wound. The river water had kept it open. In addition I was gashed and torn about the arms, legs and body where I had crashed through the thorn bush. I was worried in case the blood attracted predators. Every log began to look like a lurking crocodile. I had a feeling, even then, that I had contracted a fever. I didn't have other SAS chaps – Campbell or McNair, say – to jockey me along. When I reached the end of my tether there would be nobody to give me an extra tug, draw me on a bit further.

Night was crowding in quickly. If only I could keep going throughout the night. I doubted that Sand Shan's trackers would be able to follow a trail through occupied territory in pitch darkness. The river was quite broad now and the current was strong. What I needed was an ocean board.

The log was skewered in a tangle of roots and leaf trash. I recoiled from it at first, imagining it might be a croc. But I realised soon enough what it was and waded to it and extricated it from the tangle. It was about seven feet long, saturated and lead-heavy. The pimpling of fungus on it made my skin crawl but I forced myself to nudge it into the current and hoist myself on to it. Knees and thighs locked round it, I paddled with my hands. I couldn't use my feet because the action made my wound too painful and increased bleeding.

The surface of the river was smooth and undappled, black as bitumen. The only traces of colour lay in the sky, fading from salmon-pink to a deep velvety blue. I let the log ride out into the centre of the river and with my hands eased its slow, torpid spin to set my nose downstream. I felt utterly debilitated, sick with exhaustion. It was an effort to cling to the log, to stay awake.

Mile by mile I floated downstream. There were no signs of habitation. No signs of crocodiles, either, thank God. I felt exceedingly vulnerable, however, and cold to the bone. My wound ached and my head buzzed. I realised that I was sick from loss of blood or from swallowing too much river water. Twice I touched the bank and grounded and had to push off again. Several times I almost screamed when the log scraped floating debris or brushed against the stalks of river plants. Great hungry jaws seemed to snap at my legs. My nerves burned. Every fibre of my body hurt. What was more disturbing, I began to lose consciousness for minutes at a time.

The river took me at a lethargic pace, just another piece of flotsam which, in its own sweet time, it would spew out into the estuary.

But I was still a considerable distance from the estuary when a current carried me out of the main stream and in against the piles of a fishing pier.

I had no idea where I was – the village of Lakai Meng as it happened – or quite what was happening to me. I had a vague notion that this might be the fishing village out of which Hack Patterson's friends had been recruited. Not so. I was rubbed gently along the soggy walls of rattan traps and into a cluster of splinter-thin boats on a mud beach. The mud was soft, warmish, comfortable. I lay there, indifferently, in half sleep, bleeding, until just before dawn when a couple of young girls discovered me.

The fisherfolk of Lakai Meng might have been primitive but they weren't *that* primitive. I wasn't mistaken for a reject from the realms of the river god. They knew what I was. What's more they had been 'visited' by Jap soldiers who had stormed through the village in search of Sand Shan's guerrillas. The villagers realised that if they were caught aiding and abetting a British fugitive, the settlement would be razed to the ground and its inhabitants strung up on poles for bayonet practice.

Even so they did what they could for me. The Malays were in no way to blame for what happened.

I was semi-conscious through most of the proceedings. I was hidden out in a palm-thatch hut, my wound dressed, while the senior men of the village gathered round to decide what it would be best to do. I expect some of them thought I should be delivered to Sand Shan, but nobody knew where Shan could be located. In any case, I have subsequently discovered that the fisherfolk of the Imapoh don't much care for the Chinese and trust them only marginally more than they trust the Japs. The Chinese, apparently, moved into the fishing business in the years before the war and had creamed away the profits by tying up the market.

As I say, I was completely unaware that I was causing the villagers of Lakai Meng such a big problem. I lay on a mat, covered with a filthy blanket, in a hut perched above the river and believed myself to be still afloat. Faces came and went as in a dream. Solemn brown children and hags with pouched cheeks, and nubile girls in brightly hued sarongs came to stare at me. I suppose I was man's business, though, which is why I was put in the charge of the local *pawang*.

A *pawang* is a medicine man, an honourable enough profession as a rule. But this particular *pawang* was a fraud, a young charlatan from the swamps of Johore who was doing his rounds in the area. He gave me a sticky tea made with powdered herbs and danced and mumbo-jumboed around me, then announced – I heard and remember this – that he would take the *tuan* to the sea where the evil fever spirit would leave him and he would be restored to health. What really *is* odd is that he made his offer in English. Perhaps he had been a worker on a rubber plantation or had picked up a bit of education in Singapore. Perhaps he just wanted me to trust him and not give trouble. The herbal infusion, which almost certainly contained opium, had seen to that already.

To cut a longish story short, the Malays acted quickly. No doubt they were relieved to have the white *tuan* taken off their hands. Before the sun was properly up, I was in the bottom of a boat covered with a net and was being paddled away by two grizzled fishermen while the young *pawang* continued to chant over me.

At a place on the coast near the river mouth – I could taste the sea and hear the screeching of gulls – the *pawang* and I were offloaded and the Malays headed for home. The *pawang* gave me more of the sticky tea and told me to rest. He would bring help.

I've no idea how long he was gone, how long it took him to bargain with the Japanese commander at the post at Unghah. I wonder what he got for me. A small sack of sugar and twenty dollars cash would be about right.

All I know is that when I opened my eyes again Japanese soldiers were all around me, scowling and jabbering. And I was a prisoner of war.

2 Trademarks of terror

Big Buz Campbell made no attempt to keep in touch with Jeff Deacon or P. B. McNair after the SAS was disbanded. He heard through the grapevine, though, that Deacon had been taken prisoner by the Japanese. Later, only days before demobilisation, rumours reached the men of Deacon's squadron that the major had been found in a Jap POW camp at Seladak on Java, and was alive but all beat up. By that time P. B. McNair had gone and Buz was in the throes of figuring out his future and didn't have the chance to chase the rumour to its source.

Couple of weeks later Buz was a civvie, back in Vancouver, bored and adrift. Month after that he was logging up in the Slocan Valley, still bored if no longer adrift. But Buz never lost faith that one day the high brass in the British War Office would realise the value of having on call an élite corps of highly trained fighting men and would re-form the regiment. He just hoped to God that he wouldn't be too old before it happened.

Buz was into his eighth job and had run pretty well to seed when Jeff Deacon's letter reached him. It had been a long time on the road, re-routed through Buz's sister's home address. It finally caught up with Buz on a construction site down by Galveston where he was serving a stint as a blaster. The letter came none too soon. Another year or so of boozing and whoring and Buz wouldn't have been fit to bury never mind recruit into the Malayan Scouts, SAS, a select squadron of volunteers which was being assembled under a guy called Calvert.

The letter was terse but specific. It advised Buz to get himself to Singapore on the first available flight, to check in at the Royal Colonial Hotel and, once there, to telephone a certain Major Tim Dalinart, Calvert's deputy and right-hand man, at the new regiment's base in Johore.

'Better be quick,' Deacon advised, 'before the back door closes on geriatrics.'

Leaving nothing behind except a litter of empty beer cans, Buz

Campbell was out of Galveston within twelve hours of receipt of the letter.

A day and a half later, spruced up and neat and with his belly tucked in, Buz was seated in the cocktail bar of the Royal Colonial in Singapore with Tim Dalinart on one side of him and Jeff Deacon on the other, feeling elated, amazed and as fiery as a phoenix.

In the course of an hour's conversation with the mad, matter-of-fact Major Dalinart, Buz learned all he needed to know concerning the military situation in Malaya. He had himself a potted history lesson on the world events which had skipped by him while he was bumming around North America.

Dalinart did most of the talking.

Silently sipping a fruit juice, Jeff Deacon, who had changed almost beyond recognition, sat staring through the diamond-shaped windows of the bar into the garish haze of the street.

From Dalinart, Buz learned that the CTs – Communist terrorists – had held Malaya in thrall for over two years. Plantation owners and agents, their wives and children had been ruthlessly murdered, together with many estate workers. Terror reigned in most regions of the Peninsula. It was to strike back at the CTs, not merely to defend innocent citizens, that Special Force units had been mustered or brought back from the morgue.

Malaya provided a perfect environment for Special Force tactics. Expert in jungle fighting, Calvert had been commissioned to examine the situation and raise a unit to carry the fight into the jungles and swamps, to root out the Communists' bases, cut supply lines and kill ringleaders.

Calvert's recruiting was done mainly in Hong Kong, a garrison littered with idle soldiers. But the quality of the original intake was disappointing; 'A' Squadron was not all it might have been and did not live up to the high traditions of the SAS. Few volunteers were in shape, even fewer had jungle experience or a working knowledge of anti-guerrilla tactics. Worse, they weren't capable of surviving in brutally rough country. All in all, Dalinart explained, there were just too many 'cowboys' in the first of the élite squadrons.

It was at Deacon's suggestion that a second small-group unit of Malayan Scouts (SAS) was brought into being – 'K' Squadron.

'K' Squadron would not be responsible for training. It was an operational unit. It would be subjected to two weeks of rigorous and intensive instruction in jungle craft and the techniques of the terrorists and would then move up country on a series of deep-penetration sorties into occupied territory. It would work hand-in-glove with Special Branch officers from the Malayan Police and Security Force, with whom Deacon had been a civilian instructor prior to his re-enlistment with the SAS. 'K' Squadron operations would be experimental. Re-evaluation of its role and status in the establishment of the regiment would be done in six months, by which time, said Dalinart, 'M' Squadron would have completed its training and would have arrived, all spit and shit, from England.

'On Captain Deacon's recommendation,' said Dalinart, 'we would like you to consider joining "K" Squadron.'

'How official's the paperwork, sir?' said Buz.

'Why do you ask?'

'I'm pretty goddamned long in the tooth, and I'm not in good physical shape right now. Can *you* handle that, or is somebody back in HQ gonna carp about it and make it sticky?'

'I can handle it.'

'All right,' said Buz. 'How many officers and men will be in "K" Squadron?'

'Exactly fifty.'

'Officer Commanding?'

'I will be Officer Commanding,' said Dalinart.

'Officer in charge of operations?'

'Captain Deacon.'

Buz nodded approval.

He glanced at Deacon who, still staring from the window, did not appear to have taken in any of the talk.

Buz said, 'When's P.B. arriving?'

Deacon answered, 'He's already at Johore.'

Buz said, 'Who else have we got?'

Deacon answered, 'Nobody you know.'

'Thank Christ for that,' said Buz.

Dalinart said, 'Between us, Captain Deacon and I have personally vetted the recruits. We didn't, I might add, ask for volunteers. Captain Deacon has been working in Malaya long enough to know precisely what's required. I simply took his list of men and approached them directly.'

'Where do they come from, these guys?'

'Force 136,' said Dalinart, when Deacon seemed disinclined to reply. 'From a Rhodesian unit, from the Gurkhas, from the Malayan Police and Security forces. Even from the French Foreign Legion. An odd lot, really.'

'Odder than the old days, Jeff?' Buz asked quietly.

Deacon showed no flicker of nostalgia, no amusement.

Buz was puzzled and concerned. He had a right, really, to expect a friendly welcome from his old buddy-in-arms. Jesus, they had gone through thick and thin together in Flanders and Normandy, in Libya, Tunis, Egypt and in the ball-freezing heights of the Caucasus. And it was Deacon who had sent for him, dug him out of the gutter, along with P.B. Was there no sentiment in that? Was it plain, unvarnished efficiency? Had Deacon summoned him to Malaya, called him back into uniform just to use his talents and hard-won skills as a fighter?

'It is, I fear,' said Tim Dalinart, 'the shape of wars to come, Sergeant. What seemed odd in the German war will be the manner in which the wars of the next generation will be fought.'

Buz pondered on the change in Deacon. His blond hair was almost white and he had lost weight. He didn't appear to be sick. He was whittled down to muscle and bone, tough as rawhide. His skin was clear and tanned, in contrast to the white hair. His piercing eyes were even bluer and more icy than Buz remembered them. There were no visible scars, except for 'cuffs' of pinkish unsunned skin at each wrist, as if he had been manacled at some period. The bush shirt was clean and pressed, open at the throat. He wore the insignia of his substantive rank of Captain, having 'dropped down' from Major on re-enlistment. There were many questions Buz Campbell wanted to ask of his old buddy, but Deacon was not approachable. In fact the guy was just this side of hostile. Buz couldn't understand it.

Dalinart, on the other hand, was a cheerfully plump little guy with a fleshy nose, a badger's brush moustache and a receding hairline. He had fat useless-looking hands, almost womanish, and a less experienced recruit might have taken the Major for a fool or a fairy. But Buz had encountered the type before. One glance into the eyes was enough to tell the Canadian that he was dealing with a dedicated idealist. It gave Buz some comfort to notice that Dalinart drank strong Tom Collins, glass after glass, as if it was water. Deacon's abstemiousness was off-putting, somehow priggish.

Dalinart was saying, 'The usual training programme comprises eight weeks at the school in Kota Tinggi, which isn't far from here. But we already have an operational group working the jungle in Ipoh, quite far to the north.'

'You pick the areas where guerrilla activity is high, I guess?' said Buz.

'Quite correct. The concept is to provide a series of bases with radios for deep-penetration patrols. Pyramid style. Information on the movement of the guerrillas – let's call them CTs, which is the usual reference in these parts – on the CTs' movements is radioed out to the base HQ. Essentially, however, "K" Squadron's job is not assessment but destruction. So far the body count is abysmally low. Ferret Force and other counter-insurgent units have done sterling work but it isn't enough. Plans are well afoot to separate the guerrillas from the general population. Propaganda stuff. It need not concern you much, Sergeant. I assume you're not the sort to rampage through native villages, looting and pillaging?'

'Only back home,' said Buz.

'Winning the goodwill of the Malays is a large part of our brief,' Dalinart went on. 'We aren't dealing with a military problem in isolation. It's a social and political problem too. You must be prepared to accept that fact at the outset.'

'I've got the picture, Major,' said Buz.

'In general, you can trust the Malays.'

'But not the Chinese,' put in Deacon. 'Never trust anyone with a trace of yellow in his blood.'

'How do I tell the difference?'

'You'll learn, Sergeant,' said Dalinart.

More instruction and background were fed to Buz through Dalinart with an occasional interjection from Jeff Deacon.

Outside, the street had grown dark but through the diamond-shaped window Buz could see blobs of bright colour, like lanterns, and hear an increasing cacophony of sound which after a time seemed like a weird Chinese music.

At length Dalinart got to his feet. Buz rose too and shook the Major's hand.

Dalinart said, 'Jeff will fill in any details. Recruiting and induction processes will be done at base HQ tomorrow morning. I've laid on a jeep to bring you off the island. Carry your personal luggage with you, though you will, of course, be kitted out without delay. Don't go in much for an excess of paperwork. God knows, we have our work cut out as it is.'

Deacon, Buz noticed, remained seated.

'Cheerio, Jeff,' said Dalinart.

'Cheerio, Tim.'

'Just before you go, Major Dalinart,' said Buz, 'I've one last question.'

'Fire it,' said Dalinart.

'How long's my hitch?'

'Three years.'

'No cross-postings?'

'Exclusively with Special Air Service,' said Dalinart. 'I promise.'

'Okay,' said Buz. 'But do you figure the war'll last that long?'

'Do you want my official answer,' said Dalinart, 'or my personal and confidential opinion?'

'Your opinion, Major, please.'

Dalinart spread his soft, fat hands. 'I think we might still be fighting here in ten years' time.'

'Jesus!' said Buz. 'Are you serious?'

'He's serious,' said Jeffrey Alexander Deacon.

There was no parade ground at Johore Sambong, no mess hall, no NAAFI canteen, no buildings at all. The camp lay seven miles north-west, 'across the road' from the compounds of the official jungle warfare school. It was even more primitive in its facilities. You slept in pup tents, washed in buckets, pissed into slit trenches on the edge of the swamp-jungle and scrambled up your own grub in mess-tins over wood fires or spitting petrol stoves. You spent the morning hours lashing your body into a state of fitness, your afternoons listening to lectures on terrain and the dirty tricks of enemy forces, and evenings re-educating your shooting-arm at the 'range', in reality a couple of concrete drains attached to a pig wallow.

The separation of 'the little school' from the main base required the élite of 'K' Squadron to do their own patrol and guard duties. But after one volley of rifle-fire had scattered students, and four lethal booby-traps were uncovered in the brush along the route of the morning exercise run, chaps unused to jungle warfare began to get the idea and to work with rueful enthusiasm. Veterans all, the fifty soldiers stationed at Johore Sambong soon deduced what they were getting into and, to a man, preferred action to ease, danger to monotony.

There were five officers plus Deacon. Nineteen NCOs. The remainder were 'other ranks' including eight Malays who had been selected from a large crowd of volunteers for special skills and their hatred of the CT bandits who, like fruit flies, were turning the country rotten from the inside. Formalities associated with rank, the divisions by which the British army maintains its class structure and inculcates discipline without smothering ambition, were dispensed with in SAS 'K' Squadron. Lieutenants shared tents with buck privates, grizzled sergeant-majors shaved in the same mirror as humble corporals. It was part of Deacon's strategy, Buz Campbell reckoned, to let loyalties and friendships form of their own accord. Patrol teams would be selected more easily from men who rubbed along well together.

Deacon, however, was noticeable by his absence. He would appear infrequently, alone at the wheel of a battered jeep and hang around the training areas for a while or talk with the four training sergeants or a couple of the lieutenants, then vanish again. He gave Buz and P.B. no special attention during the fortnight and only recognised their presence with a curt nod.

'Didn't he say nothin', Buz,' P. B. McNair would ask, 'when you met him in Singapore?'

'Hardly a goddamned word. Asked me how I'd been, like he didn't much care,' Buz answered. 'Snuck off into the night about ten minutes after Dalinart.'

'Same here,' said P.B. 'Wouldn't even stay for a bloody drink. Says he doesn't drink much any more. Christ, who'd have thought it! The Deke gone dry on us.'

'He was with the Malayan cops, right?'

'Aye. Yon wee dark joker, Cho Pye, he was with the same outfit and trained under the Deke.'

'Have you chinned the Malay about Jeff?'

'The Malay won't talk. Just smiles.'

'It sure ain't like it was,' said Buz. 'If I'd known it was gonna be like this, maybe I'd have stayed in Galveston.'

'Aye, like hell y'would!'

Buz grinned. 'Right, wee man. Right. I'd have friggin' walked to Singapore to escape from civvy street.'

In material terms civilian life had not been hard on Peter Bennet McNair. He had done all right for himself. He had even begun to sink into a kind of respectability. On demob he had not returned to his native city of Glasgow. He had settled in London, found a job with the catering staff of the LMS railway company and had wound up as a Pullman car attendant on night express sleepers. An equable temperament kept P.B. in the job, though half the time he was pickled in whisky. He even managed to meet and marry the elder daughter of an LMS guard without ever attaining complete sobriety. He and Alice moved into the back bedroom of his in-laws' council house in Paddington, where Alice still lived along with P.B.'s daughter, 'a bonnie wee lassie' named after her mother. The child was the only item in the accumulated dross of the four-year post-war period that P.B. valued and that had given him a moment's hesitation when Deacon's letter arrived.

'I tell you, Buz, I even sobered up for a week, such a bloody shock it gave me.'

'But you came.'

'I'm here. Right?'

'What did she say when you told her you were leavin'? Your missus.'

' "Good riddance" was what she said. She gets the lion's share of ma pay, an' she's better wi' that than wi' me.'

'And the kid?'

P.B. frowned. 'Ach, she'll be okay.'

'You'll see her again, when the tour's over. Right?'

'Aye, right.' said P. B. McNair.

There was no mystery as to what lay behind Buz Campbell's desire to be back in the uniform of the SAS or of P. B. McNair's sacrifice of a monotonous existence as a railway servant. Only Deacon remained an enigma, an interesting – almost fascinating – topic of conversation while the burly sergeant and wiry little corporal pounded the 'loop' in the cool of the morning, their shorts and khaki vests sodden with the toxins of four years of self-indulgence, their feet aching in black gym pumps. They were too crafty to allow themselves to be caught in the fierce competitiveness which Training Sergeant Muscroft whipped up in the younger men, eager tigers who thought that being first back to the shit-pole every morning meant they were the best soldiers in the unit, whose tapered waists and smooth muscles made such a contrast with Buz's hairy bulk and P.B.'s string-like frame.

Campbell and McNair ran at their own pace. Muscroft kept off their necks, noting by the stopwatch in his horny hand that every morning, without fail, the pair completed the fourteen laps of the circuit in a faster time and reckoning rightly that they knew what they were doing when it came to building fitness for the work they would soon have to do. Besides, Muscroft had seen Campbell and McNair handle the ordnance, had marvelled at the teamwork and the speed with which they could strip and reassemble weapons and the lethal accuracy they brought to free shooting at the range. There was nothing that range-sergeant and weapons instructor Burch could teach them except to impart a few wrinkles on the Japanese guns which the CTs used.

Fourteen nights under canvas, a dozen of them wet, put nobody off their fodder. Rations were generous, the quality of the food excellent. There were experiments with 'exotic' local fruits and vegetables and a forty-eight-hour course in 'jungle edibles', which mainly consisted of fern tips, certain types of fungi and mosses, and in learning how to peel bamboo shoots with your teeth.

The crash training programme was suddenly over. The unit was mustered at five in the afternoon in the shade of a large awning slung on ropes in the centre of the camp area. The men were addressed cheerfully by Major Tim Dalinart then by Captain Jeff Deacon whose demeanour was businesslike and grim.

'You may imagine,' Deacon began, 'that you have learned a great deal in the course of the past two weeks, but you have learned nothing. Malayan jungles and swamps and the bandits that live therein will teach you humility and patience and the fact that one can never tread too warily in this country at this time. You will learn very quickly – or you will not survive. None of you is without experience in small-group raid and assault operations. You have been accepted – invited – to join this squadron because of your expertise. And for one purpose. That purpose is not just to protect the lives and property of rubber planters and their employees but to hunt down and to kill terrorists.'

'I ain't sure the C-in-C would approve of this speech,' Buz whispered to P. B.

Captain Deacon went on for twenty minutes. The men under the awning listened intently. Deacon made their position plain. No frills. No bullshit. Within twenty-four hours they would be in the jungle, hunting CTs. They were after the big shots, Deacon explained, command bases, arms dumps, CT training camps in the jungle.

' "K" Squadron has a particular target,' Deacon said. 'One guerrilla leader. He's been operating between Taluk and Kuala Lumpur, a large stretch of country. He's well supplied and armed and has a considerable number of trained Chinese under his command. He keeps a low profile, however, and steers clear of the Malayan Communist Party. There's reason to believe that he receives financial support from certain Chinese "fat cats" – businessmen. He tends not to curry favour with backwoods villagers but to extort what he needs from them by force. He's slippery, very slippery, and utterly without scruples. This particular Chink is our target. His name is Wei Sand Shan.'

Deacon paused. The awning moved above the gathering as the cooling air came up from the swamp country to the east of the encampment.

'I want him,' Deacon said. 'I want him dead or alive.'

'I reckon he means it,' said big Buz Campbell.

'With knobs on,' said P. B. McNair.

'Now, Shan has an excellent intelligence network. The damned country is riddled with his spies. You saw the booby-traps, heard the gunfire. Not a serious attempt to frighten us, just a little warning. Our base is prepared for us, a permanent camp in a meadow near the township of Port Kernan. It's a hundred and eighty miles up the coast from Kuala Lumpur, beyond Kuala Selangor, on the border of Perak. Rubber country lies around it to the south and south-east. Reports give strong indication that Shan has a headquarters in that area. I intend to flush him out. What's more,' the Captain continued, 'I intend to do it at speed, to give Shan's spies and informers no opportunity to read our hand.'

'Uh-huh! This don't sound comfortable,' murmured Buz.

'Maps, please.'

A Gurkha sergeant carried a metal easel from behind the bench platform on which Deacon stood. He unfolded it and set it up beside the Captain, brought a large map board to which maps were spring-clipped from the rear of the area and pegged it to the easel.

Deacon waited with a patience that was reflected in the men below him. There wasn't much talk. Cigarettes were lighted hurriedly. They had all attended briefings before and knew that what was said would affect them greatly during the course of the next few days. In addition there was something so intense about the Captain that the soldiers took him seriously and with a faint undertone of apprehension.

Deacon used no pointer. He stood to one side of the easel and rapped the carefully drawn map with his forefinger nail.

'The west coastline of Malaya. Four-hundred-odd miles of it. We're down here, on the tip of the Peninsula, just above Singapore. Here is Port Kernan, and this is the general area in which we believe Wei Sand Shan will be found. The red stars, by the way, indicate CT attacks and murders.'

'Busy little bastard, ain't he?'

'The area is too sprawling to be effectively protected, though many plantation workers have been brought into compounds and the Malayan Police have done sterling work within the limits of their manpower.' Deacon tapped the map again. 'This railway line links Singapore to Kuala Lumpur. Two-forty, two-fifty miles of it. It extends up to Kuala Selangor along the coast. It's by that railway that we will travel to Port Kernan.' Deacon paused. 'Some of us.'

'Uh-huh!' said Buz again, under his breath. 'Wait for the punchline.'

'Believe me when I say that Wei Sand Shan will know our travel plans. He will be kept abreast of our departure and our arrival. He may even prepare some kind of welcome for us. Probably on the road between Kuala Selangor and Port Kernan. He will have units on the jungle edge already. He will be keen to show us what he's made of, to ruffle our feathers. But with all that cover at his back he will think he's safe.'

Deacon switched maps; a hand-drawn job showed the west and central area in detail.

'Can you all see?'

'We're beginnin' to, Captain,' Buz called.

Deacon nodded, without a smile.

His forefinger traced the line of the railway. 'We board the milk run, the daily service train between Singapore and KL, here at Johore Bharu. Three additional passenger coaches and an extra goods van will have been added to the make-up to accommodate us. We'll be very comfortable.' Again Deacon paused. Again Deacon added, 'Some of us.'

'Captain,' said P.B., 'is this the old back-door dodge?'

'Is it that obvious, Corporal McNair?'

'Only if you've seen it before,' McNair answered.

'I do hope you're right,' said Deacon. 'I wouldn't wish to deliver forty men straight into Wei Sand Shan's hands.'

'Well, sir, unless this Chinkie joker was scuffin' round Sedan in nineteen-forty-four,' said P.B., 'he'll no' guess what we're up to – if it's done right.'

Deacon nodded and returned to the easel.

'It *will* be done right. The element of surprise is crucial. So far, surprise has been one of the CTs' main weapons. Now it's our turn. Wei Sand Shan will know that a detachment of SAS is on its way from here. He'll have the tally soon after we embark. Believe me, his intelligence is that good. Fifty soldiers will disembark at KL and retrain there for the last leg to Kuala Selangor where trucks will be waiting to run them to Port Kernan. Point is that the fifty soldiers who get on the train at Johore Bharu won't be the same fifty who climb out at KL.'

Buz glanced round the assembled soldiers. Some were grinning quite openly. Cunning appealed to them. Buz was guarded, though. From what he could see of the map there was a lot of goddamned green stuff between the railway junction and the three blue markers which, he guessed, represented their objectives.

Deacon said, 'On board the train will be fifty troops from "A" Squadron. They are only going along for the trip and will spend only a week or so at Port Kernan, warming up the beds for us. A week should be long enough to see us into our positions.'

One corporal, a bull-necked youngster, ex-Para, ex-wrestler, named Norman Paul, raised his hand. 'Won't Shan recognise some of you by sight, sir?'

'He might – just – recognise me or Major Dalinart.'

'I'll be with the transit unit, in any case,' put in Dalinart.

'The rest of you have been deliberately kept out of circulation. To the Chinese you are just uniforms, not faces,' said Deacon. 'We'll leave the train in three groups, in the middle of nowhere. We'll have travelled in the spare goods van, well out of sight. Not even railway porters will know quite what's going on. Our training sergeants will not be with us on this exercise.'

An ironic cheer went up, stifled as soon as Deacon raised his hand.

Deacon said, 'We will operate from the drop points in three distinct and separate groups. Radio communication will not be possible on this occasion but, for reference purposes, the groups will be designated by the code names "Gable", "Tracy" and "Flynn".'

Laughter greeted this information. Hollywood tough-guys did not seem inappropriate. Buz reckoned that the names had been chosen by Dalinart, however, not Deacon, who did not share in the general amusement but waited solemnly for the laughter to subside.

'Each group will be accompanied by at least one Malay-speaker and by two men who know the territory. The first group, "Flynn", will be under the command of Lieutenant Sherret. The second, "Tracy", will be led by Captain Silverwood. These will be fairly large units, eighteen men in each, plus trackers. I will be in charge of "Gable"; a smaller group. Names of personnel in group divisions will be posted after this briefing.'

Deacon turned down the third and last map on the easel. It showed the area west of the railway in greater detail still. Quite artistic, Buz thought, with little bungalows and rubber plantations neatly drawn, and certain areas of vegetation emblemised. It still looked like one hell of a long way.

'You will carry weapons, of course, plus jungle kit, plus rations. There will be the usual medical emergency packs and water purification tablets. Pretty heavy burdens for your first jungle foray but very necessary,' Deacon continued. ' "Flynn" and "Tracy" will have a pretty easy trek of about forty miles apiece and should, I'm told, manage this in three days.'

'Three days, Captain?' asked one of the older officers, a former Desert Rat, who had been used to covering that sort of distance in a single day.

'Three days is a conservative estimate,' said Deacon. 'You haven't experienced the Malayan hinterland yet, have you, Hornby?'

'Haven't had that pleasure,' Lieutenant Hornby replied.

'It will take three days, even for tigers like you,' Deacon said. ' "Flynn" will head directly down the Selsing Valley, where there is an elephant trail, and will hole out at the back of the MacArthur rubber plantation. "Tracy" will tackle a horseshoe route, avoiding the road at Jorong, here, and will take position on the hill overlooking the plantation at Taris.'

Buz held up his hand.

'Sergeant Campbell?'

'Do the planters know we're coming?'

'Yes and no,' said Deacon.

'I've heard they're pretty nervy and liable to pop off at anything that moves,' said Buz.

'They have been told only that there may be security patrols in their neck of the woods next week. I imagine that may make them slightly circumspect about twitching the trigger. But in effect it's rather up to us to make sure we aren't spotted even by the planters and the tappers. The concept of the operation is centred on the fact that Wei Sand Shan's guerrillas will be caught in the act.'

'Why these particular locations, Captain?'

'They are remote. Natural targets. Indeed, all three have been subjected to constant vicious harrassment. Natives have been slaughtered and attempts have been made on the lives of the managers and their families.'

'Why don't the Europeans just pack up and get out?'

Dalinart answered. 'Because they're British. And stubborn. They refuse to be browbeaten into giving up their jobs and their life-style. They may be afraid, but they are proud. And they detest the Communist method.'

Deacon continued, 'I've studied Wei Sand Shan's methods and his psychology. When Shan learns that an SAS unit has been moved on to the border of his area, that we're giving him special attention, he won't skulk off into hiding. He'll give us a show, a gesture of defiance. "A" Squadron may pick up some of this flak – I wouldn't be surprised – but my guess is that Shan will order his guerrillas to commit an act or acts of particular barbarism. He will endeavour to wipe out one or all of the plantations which we'll be guarding.'

'But we'll have gone in by the back door, as the Corporal pointed out, and Shan's terrorists won't be up against a civilian or two with a pair of rifles or a shotgun and a few trained guard-dogs. They'll find themselves in a fight; a genuine fight,' said Tim Dalinart. 'And they won't like that one little bit.'

'If any of the raiders escape,' said Deacon, 'we'll trail them. We'll track them down. We'll be in *their* territory this time and they won't have their usual start.'

'How will this help us nail Shan?' Hornby asked.

'Perhaps it won't,' said Deacon. 'But it will reduce his forces and teach him he can't flout military and security forces without loss. And, of course, if we capture prisoners they might be persuaded to tell us where Shan is hidden.'

'Is that likely?' said Buz Campbell.

'Quite likely,' said Deacon. 'Only the hard core of the guerrillas are dedicated. Rank and file CTs are often pressed men or in it for the prestige or the profit. Not committed to the Communist cause.'

'Anything else you'd like to know, chaps?' said Dalinart.

'Sir, will we be comin' back here when the operation's over?'

Deacon answered, 'No. You've seen the last of Johore Sambong.'

Another murmured cheer.

Buz raised his voice. 'You haven't told us yet where "Gable" is headed, sir.'

'I prefer to keep that information up my sleeve.'

'Any special reason, sir?'

'No, no special reason,' said Deacon. 'I'll tell you once we're on our way.'

'We?'

'Yes,' said Deacon.

Buz grinned. Cold and distant Deacon might be but he hadn't yanked his old buddies off civvy street just to sweat round the loop or tote a Sten at the gates of Port Kernan. Buz glanced at P.B. The Scot had picked up the implication too. He gave the sergeant a big wink. Yeah, it was going to be the three of them after all; Deacon, Campbell and McNair. Like in the old days.

Poor old bloody Wei Sand Shan. The bastard wouldn't know what hit him.

At 05.00 hours the following morning the men of 'K' Squadron roused themselves and assembled quietly for the march to the rail halt at Johore Bharu. At 07.00 hours precisely the quaint green and red train steamed alongside the low platform and the troops swarmed into the empty passenger carriages. They didn't make themselves comfortable, however, but as soon as the train got up steam picked their way in threes down the corridors and across the rattling bridge to the inner goods van, to be replaced by uniformed soldiers from the SAS 'A' Squadron. In less than an hour the change-over had been effected and Deacon's élite settled down in the stifling gloom of the goods van to endure the six-hour trip.

It was sometime around 13.30 hours when the train squealed to a halt. The rear door of the van was dragged open and 'Flynn' went over the bridge and vanished into the undergrowth by the track side.

Ten minutes later the train stopped again, and 'Tracy' took to the jungle.

Five men were left in the goods van. One of these was the 'dispatcher', a Corporal Abelman. In addition to the Captain and P.B., there was big Buz Campbell and a small dark-skinned Gurkha who introduced himself as Johnny Badhur and who wore the same rank markings as Buz. He held out his hand.

Buz and P.B. shook it in turn.

'Where'd you learn to fight, Johnny?' P.B. asked.

'Same as you,' Badhur answered. 'Middle East. I was with the Second Battalion of the 4th, old fellow, at Tobruk.'

'And later in India and Burma,' said Deacon.

'Long time in Burma,' Badhur added.

'Kill many Japs?' asked P.B., one hunter to another.

'Not enough,' said Johnny Badhur.

Seated on the floor of the van – the train had picked up speed again – Buz said, 'Is this it, Jeff?'

'Plus one Dyak tracker who we'll meet in the jungle.'

Minutes later the train ground to a halt once more and the four SAS troopers slid their packs out of the door and dropped after them between the sleepers of the gravel track.

A little stiff after the cramped trip, Buz found himself last into the brush, the huge Bergen rucksack and an oilcloth gun-sack cradled in his arms. Crouching, the Canadian watched the train pull out with crisp, clean puffs of white steam issuing from its cylinders and brown smoke from its stack. There were no heads in the windows, no guards hanging from the van bridge. Nobody to wave them goodbye. Jungle swallowed the train up like a python will swallow a mouse.

The track ran north and south in a shallow curve. All else was jungle, dense, green, impacted.

Buz glanced at P.B., who shrugged. It had come home to the Canadian and the Scot how little they knew of this strange land and how goddamned inhospitable it was to strangers. Neither of them would have known where to begin the trek, how to tackle the breast-high tangle of vegetation or to read the trees.

Badhur seemed quite at home. Deacon too. The Captain was smiling. It wasn't much of a smile and it seemed to sit stiffly on his mouth but it was a sign at last that there was still some pleasure in life and not just duty. The Deke was happy, Buz reckoned, to be shot of the trappings of the barracks, the last contact with civilisation. You couldn't even smell the lingering wisps of train smoke now, only the hot salty odour of the jungle overlaid with the sweetness of unseen flowers. Deacon got to his feet and stretched. Puffing out his cheeks he emptied his lungs and filled them again. He was, Buz thought, like a bull released from winter quartering, or a wolf from its cage.

'Now what, Jeff?' asked Buz.

'Now,' said Deacon, 'there's nobody around to remind us that this is not a war but an "emergency". We're free to fight the way we've been trained to do.'

'Too true, boss,' said Johnny Badhur. 'Now we can go to get Sand Shan.'

'Right, sure,' said Buz. 'But which way?'

'That way,' said Deacon, pointing into the thorns.

*

After an hour hacking his way through leaves and vines, enveloped in a cloud of tiny gnat-like insects, the jungle of Malaya had lost its magic for P. B. McNair.

They had covered about a quarter of a mile, he figured. Nothing had changed. The trees looked the same, the 'cabbage' looked the same and the bloody, blood-thirsty cloud of insects seemed to have settled around them permanently.

P.B. had always been happiest when he could move freely. Quick-witted, fast on his pins, not reduced in nimbleness by his years as a Pullman porter, he rapidly decided that the jungle was not his kind of environment. He was stifled by it, throttled, felt if he had to swing the *parang*, a heavy, long-bladed knife, much longer his fuckin' arm would drop off. It wasn't the trek but the hedge-cutting that wore you out.

The Bergen was tight and comfortable but it hadn't been designed to be worn by a joker chopping through green shit. The strap rubbed and skinned the neck tendons on the left side. A swipe or sweep wasn't enough to hack a path through the stuff. You had to take a full swing, using back and body muscles too. The string-like creepers which stitched the leaves of the ground plants together were tough as wire. The Gurkha told him they were a species of climbing palms known as rattans, mixed in with *palas*. *Bertam* was the stemless, spiny garbage which seemed to have been deliberately planted to make the going not only tough but painful.

Frankly, P.B. didn't give a fuck what the jungle was composed of or how it would change when they cleared the dry rim along which the railway had been built. He had a nasty suspicion that it would change for the worse. Anyhow, at the rate they were travelling, they'd be bloody lucky to clear the 'dry rim' by Christmas. Neither the Deke nor the Gurkha took compass readings. They just plunged on, pushing in what may or may not have been a straight line. To P.B. it seemed crazy, an ultimate sort of SAS lunacy and one to which he could not lend enthusiasm. He did his stint with the blade for ten or fifteen minutes up front of the quartet, then was replaced by one of the others and dropped to the rear. Unwrapping his rifle, he carried it at the port, but God knew what he was supposed to do with it or what he was supposed to fire at since he couldn't see further than two yards in any direction and barely had space to shoulder the bloody weapon.

Badhur told him that they were now in monkey country.

'How do you know, Johnny?'

'I can smell 'em, Pete.'

P.B. could smell all sorts of things but which particular odour told the Gurkha that there were monkeys about he hadn't a clue. It wasn't that he didn't believe the guy. In fact, as he grew used to the surroundings, his senses sharpened, like your eyes growing accustomed to the dark, and he saw all sorts of things he hadn't noticed before; a zoo of different sorts of insects in the undergrowth – ants, of course, and spiders, tiny lizards, centipedes. The joint was fairly jumpin'. Apart from an occasional whistle or cry, however, it was so quiet you'd have thought the jungle had been struck with blight. Come to think of it, the bloody jungle *was* the blight.

Buz was up front. The Canadian wielded the *parang* with quickly acquired expertise. He'd been a logger so maybe he knew what he was doing. Backhand, forehand and a sort of uppercut – and the way was clear enough for Buz to thrust his chest and belly through, find another tangle to cut away. On and on, with only two standing halts for water out of the bottle and a fast drag on a fag.

But the Deke seemed happy, comfortable here in the deep green underworld. However thin he'd become, he hadn't lost his stamina. He did his stint with the blade with a kind of economy, an almost surgical precision, and parted the torn vines and leaves with a delicate touch.

It was three and a half hours after they had left the railway line before P.B. noticed an appreciable change in the density of the growth.

'Arrive soon,' said Johnny Badhur.

'Arrive where?' growled P.B.

Johnny smiled and held up his thumb. He turned again and waded after Deacon who was to the front, breaking trail.

The going became easier. They must have been making half a mile an hour in the last stretch. Even P.B. could tell they were coming to something. He had a vision of a fine big pub plonked by an asphalt road, its doors open in welcome and its fans wafting out the rich smell of beer. When he closed his eyes he thought he could smell the brew. He wasn't wrong about the niff, only about the source of it.

The Deke parted branches – and there was the lake.

There seemed to be no shore to speak of, just a strip of festering, blistered mud the colour of horse manure, with a scatter of birds on it dabbing and pecking. The water looked more like jelly than liquid, the colour of an army vest. Knitted round its flatness was more bloody jungle. It was the lake that smelled like fermented hops. But at least one wee riddle had been explained; Deacon had cut straight in from the railway line, knowing full well he must strike the lake shore. He had five or six miles of leeway which on a five-mile hike was a big margin for error.

The sun laid a rusty band on the trees on the far bank which couldn't have been more than a half-mile away. P.B. could see things in the trees, grey mobile shapes; Badhur's monkeys like as not. Lots of birds, including pigeons, which were familiar enough to give P.B. a sudden fleeting longing to be back home in a friendly city now that it was opening time and the sun was waning.

Big Buz Campbell was probably thinking the same sort of thing.

'Can we drink it?' Buz nodded towards the lake.

Deacon replied, 'Lord, no. We'll find a clean pool or a stream soon. But don't drink anything without putting a chlorine tablet in it first.'

Treading carefully, Deacon went forward out of the undergrowth. He was protected on either flank by the trunks of tall, clean trees which had a dithering mass of tiny red leaves growing upon their lower limbs. Buz and P.B. instinctively clasped their rifles tightly and stepped out to form a rear flank. If there was space, P.B. assumed, there was room for a Commie bullet to find you, since any stretch of water in this blighted country would attract more than local fauna.

Accompanied by a chittering mass of smaller birds, waders deserted the mud flat, beating up and away across the water. Off to his right P.B. saw three cow-like creatures of a light rust colour with horns as long as trombones trample out of a wallow and crash into the jungle.

Deacon stopped where he was for a couple of minutes, Johnny Badhur right behind him, a Sten held across his chest, slender, tobacco-coloured finger on the trigger.

'Well,' said Deacon, 'I imagine that Umgah will know we've arrived.'

'Umgah's the tracker, right?' said Buz.

'Dyak,' Johnny Badhur explained. 'Originally from North Borneo. Worked with the OSS in the war and came across the channel with the units to track here. Been here ever since.'

'So where is he?'

'Under the mahogany trees,' said Deacon.

There was a sound in the air like frying bacon. The mud strip was alive with mosquitoes and other flying insects which, stirred by the flight of the birds, seeped up and settled about the soldiers.

'Look,' said Deacon. 'You can see the structure of the jungle very well from here.'

Obediently Buz and P.B. stared across the lake.

Deacon said, 'The taller the upper layer of trees the easier the going beneath them. Light is the governing factor in the growth of ground plants and brush. There are four layers or storeys. The top storey grows to a couple of hundred feet, large trees which form into a canopy that keeps out the light from beneath them and inhibits the growth of the other three storeys of vegetation.'

'Is this a lesson, Deke?' Buz asked.

'This is a lesson,' Deacon said. 'Tall trees mean faster going. What we've come through is dense second-grade forest. The undergrowth springs up faster when it has more light and air, where the big trees are scarce.'

'We have come down hill,' said Johnny Badhur. 'Very gradual slope off the dry rim. Across the lake it is mixed timber all the way to the fringe of the rubber plantations.'

'What's this about mahogany?'

'We've to look for a stand of mahogany timber,' said Deacon. 'There we will rendezvous with the tracker.'

'How does he know what day and time it is?'

'He doesn't,' said Deacon. 'He'll have been here for three, four, five days.'

'Jesus!' said Buz Campbell. 'Doin' what?'

Deacon shrugged. 'Curing one of his trophies perhaps.'

'Trophies?'

'Heads.'

'You mean . . .?'

'Human heads, yes. That's Umgah's price. Not dollars, not bullets, not even a nice shiny Woolworth's wristwatch. Each time he leads us to a kill he gets himself another trophy.'

P.B. swallowed and felt sweat start afresh down his backbone. 'How . . . how many "trophies" has this joker got?'

'Twenty-five or thirty,' said Deacon. 'He'll be a highly respected gentleman when he returns to his village in Borneo.'

'You're pullin' my string, Deke.'

'I'm not, you know.'

'And you . . . you let him have them?'

Deacon laughed drily. 'Why should I stop him? My only inflexible rules are that the owner of the head must be Chinese and unquestionably dead.'

Badhur interrupted. 'There, boss. Mahogany trees.'

'So it is. So it is,' said Deacon. 'Come along. It's probably safe enough to go around the lake edge. We're too deep for CTs. No targets for them here.'

'If we are lucky, Pete,' said Johnny Badhur to the little Scots corporal, 'Umgah will have tea ready for us to eat.'

'Tea?' said P.B.

'In a manner of speaking,' said Johnny Badhur

Elephants had come down to the lake to drink in the cool of the afternoon. There were about twenty of them, cows mostly, some with calf at heel. One big-tusked bull rode shotgun on the herd. In Kinta and Perak and other cultivated areas of the Peninsula the elephant was a domestic animal, tamed and harnessed for haulage and land-clearance. But in the wild, Badhur informed P.B., they were not to be tampered with.

P.B. took the Gurkha's word for it. What surprised him about the animals was their violence. Maybe they were enjoying themselves there in the muddy waters but their bulk gave them menace; and they were fast. Slashing trunks and bargings of the heads, tramplings, all the time the bellowing and steam-train hissings and puffings.

'Keep away,' said Johnny Badhur again.

What the hell did the Gurkha think he was going to do? Walk up and offer the bull a bun?

The presence of the elephant herd on the lake shore meant a wide detour or a long wait; the animals wouldn't leave the wallow until after dusk. The going, though, was easier and there were trails of sorts, one of which cut across the elephant track, a swathe of devastation which the herd had cut on its drive to the water and which reminded P.B. of the sort of havoc a Churchill tank could wreak in a cornfield.

The young spiny palm plants had been crushed flat and flies packed the juicy remnants, moving like unfastidious diners from milky ooze to the steaming heaps of dung which marked the elephants' passage through the jungle. Torn creepers and uprooted bushes and ugly black thorn trees yanked out like tufts of hair made quite a clearway and let the waning sun shaft down through the cathedral-like trees. The soldiers had crossed the elephant track, two or three hundred yards from the lake shore. Though he could see nothing of the herd, the noise was loud, like traffic on a bottleneck at Oxford Street. Bringing up the rear, P.B. was barely past the last fly-coated turd when instinct made him turn round.

The Deke and Buz Campbell had already vanished into trembling leaves. If the Gurkha had been a pace or two quicker he would have been gone too and P.B. in weary panic might have acted on first impulse and put a bullet through the native's head.

P.B. would never forget it. He had encountered more than his share of primitive peoples in North Africa and the remoter regions of peasant France, but the sight of the Dyak standing there in hazy sunlight, coke-coloured and small, barrel-chested and flat-nosed, naked except for an immodest leathery ball-bag, plunged the Scots corporal instantly into another world, into a time before history. He was possessed by awe and a sense of wonderment which caused him to hold the shot.

The native carried two spears, one short and one long, and had a knife-sheath slung across his muscular chest. He made no movement, did not shy away when P.B. spotted him, not even when P.B. jerked up the rifle. It was the dark man's utter lack of motion which stayed the corporal.

For a moment the two warriors stared at each other, both scowling very slightly but not at all unsure, not now. There was, in a bizarre fashion, rapport between them. P. B. McNair too was small, swarthy and simian. He too had learned the knack of standing completely still. The elephants' jamboree went on and Johnny Badhur vanished after the others into the jungle.

P.B. didn't smile. He shifted the rifle, tucking the butt under his right arm, and made the one and only gesture he could think of under the circumstances, the old picture-house cliché coming home to roost in reality at last.

He held up his left hand, palm out, and intoned, 'Me friend.'

Nothing happened. The carbon-tinted idiot just stared at him.

P.B. said, 'You Umgah. Right?'

The Dyak giggled, grinned and nodded. 'Me. Me Umgah. Rightio, *tuan*. Rightio. Rightio.'

The joker came forward, still grinning – much teeth, *tuan* – and shook his crossed spears at P.B. who, out of formal courtesy, lowered the rifle about one inch.

'Friend. Friend. Carparal, me friend. Rightio. Carparal got smoke?'

'Smoke?'

The sign was unmistakable, like a bloody Abdullah advert; the empty vee of the Dyak's fingers carried to his mouth, the puff, the blowing out of imaginary smoke and a sigh of satisfaction. Christ, thought P.B. ruefully, here I am meetin' a head-hunter in the heart of the bloody jungle and the first thing the bastard does is bum a fag off of me.

'Aye, sure,' said P. B. McNair and, putting the rifle between his knees, dug out his tobacco tin.

Deacon to Holms: August 1951

Unsure that Campbell or McNair would take to jungle warfare and uncertain as to what effect four years of civilian comfort might have had upon their morale I deliberately kept them at a distance. Between Calvert, Dalinart and me there was an unwritten agreement that unsuitable recruits to the élite squadrons would be pruned out at the end of the first phase of the operations. Chums or not, I had no wish to deceive Campbell and McNair into thinking that they were being offered a sinecure or that they would be carried by the re-formed regiment on the strength of their career records. They would have to prove themselves to me, and our first 'deep end' dive into the worst possible jungle without support would, I felt, make or break them.

The appearance of the Dyak, his affinity with McNair, somehow strengthened my conviction that my play was a good one; the more so when the Dyak told me that Wei Sand Shan in person had trekked forty armed bandits along the lake shore only two days before, heading for the plantations to the north-east.

They had been travelling quickly, the Dyak claimed, and were accompanied by coolie bearers laden with rattan packs. They had passed along an elephant track not half a mile from the Dyak's *basha*. He had dismantled his leaf shelter and buried his fire, though he feared they might smell the fish he had been smoking at the time.

Was he sure of the number?

'Eight hands, Keptin *tuan*,' he told me.

McNair nodded as if to support his new-found friend.

'Was Wei Sand Shan with the men for sure?'

Much scowling and nodding and circled fingers and thumbs over the eyes to signify the terrorist leader's spectacles.

The Dyak was an excellent observer. I had worked with him on previous occasions on patrol with Special Branch (Intelligence) foot-sloggers in Perak. The Dyak had no love for the Chinese. He made little differentiation between the settlers and the CTs, classifying them all, men, women and children, as his enemies and referring to them sometimes as 'Nips', a slip which nobody bothered to correct.

Dyaks all parleyed pidgin Malayan, the lingua franca of the Straits Settlements and the majority of the islands of the Archipelago. Our Dyak, however, had been with soldiers since he was a stripling and had mastered the patois of the barracks pretty well. But his tongue distorted the words, particularly vowels. It took a little practice to follow his conversation. McNair, a Glaswegian born and bred, seemed to experience no difficulty in communication, however. Within an hour of making contact he was jawing away nineteen to the dozen with the tribesman.

My inclination, as you may imagine, was to hare off in pursuit of the bloody little terrorist. But haste would have been ill-advised. Already the jungle was beginning to take its toll on Campbell and McNair. Besides, Wei Sand Shan had nowhere to go. We had three parties in the jungle and one of them, with a little luck, would net him this time.

The Dyak had prepared a dry, snug *basha* for us in the roots of the mahogany trees. No ants, no rats, he assured me. He had also gone to rather a lot of bother to lay on a feast of welcome. It was a paste of cold rice and smoked fish stuffed into bamboo tubes which he proceeded to bake over a hot-stone fire. He had filled coconuts with fresh water. All in all, he was a very friendly Dyak.

On the slog for fourteen hours, we were all dead beat. Even Johnny seemed glad to sit down and take off his boots. He had only recently recovered from a nasty attack of foot-rot and the skin was still tender. He poured a little fresh water on to a scarf and held it against his aching toes, crooning with relief. I told them we would eat and rest and recommence the trek at first light.

McNair had a bottle of Scotch in his pack. We had a snifter before supper. The jungle was fragrant and the rumpus that the elephant herd made seemed friendly. The monkeys that Johnny had smelled swung past. Gibbons, I think. They hesitated in the goat-trees on our flank, gibbering and gossiping. I could feel the calming effect of dusk and remoteness coming upon me. There was no wire here, no reeking streets or noisy *kampongs* to remind me of anything.

We finished supper with fresh pineapple.

I told Buz Campbell he mustn't expect such luxury very often and that it was the Dyak we had to thank for it. Unlike McNair, Buz was wary of the Dyak.

We lingered over tea, brewed almost black and taken with handfuls of sugar. We didn't talk much. Buz was keen to mull over the 'old days'. He would probably have tried to wheedle me into telling him what had happened to me at the hands of the Japanese. But that, as you know, is a boring tale. The only point of interest is why they didn't execute me but sent me instead to Java after trying to beat the truth about Sand Shan's raid out of my fevered bones. Perhaps the mystery of how I survived would provide a suitably philosophic topic for post-prandial chat – but not in that company.

I tell myself that I was preserved by fate to mete out punishment on Wei Sand Shan; and that will do for a simple soldier who has lost his faith in duty, will it not?

Fully clad and wrapped in proofed ponchos, we slept well enough. The Dyak was wrong about the rats. Quite a pack of them invaded the camp after dark. I could hear their stealthy rustlings and squeaks of delight as they discovered the pile of charred bamboos in which supper had been cooked. The crunching of teeth was like a lullaby, however, for I was sleepy and full of confidence that I had Sand Shan right where I wanted him.

At first light we were up. Johnny stirred us a pot of maize porridge while Campbell and McNair checked and cleaned the guns. Oilcloth carry-sacks or not, humidity can play havoc with tooled weapons and one can almost watch rust form on stainless steel.

The wailing of gibbons jeered us away from the tail of the lake and along the spidery path which the Dyak had scouted in advance and which lay on a line parallel with Sand Shan's route.

All morning we trekked. There was no cutting to do, however, and we made exceptional progress.

Johnny was the only problem. His feet were hurting again, even if he was too proud to admit it. It was unusual for a Gurkha to have hoof trouble, but *lupus vulgaris* is no respecter of persons. When we stopped for a breather, he would go into the bush with his pack, to dust the toes with a dermacidal powder which seemed to do some good.

There is little to say about the walk, about that day or the next. We spent the night on a dry ledge among palms after a cold supper from the ration packs, and headed on again, travelling north-east.

When one surveys the map of Malaya it seems such a small country, nothing compared to the vast biscuits of empty space on the North African charts. It seems to have character and variety and a cosiness, which in the interior is not at all the case. The jungle consumes, digests and regurgitates everything. Only the fast traveller remains – comparatively – immune to its cankers.

The Dyak kept us going. Undoubtedly he could have outstripped us by many a mile if he had wished but we were paying him and he had learned just the right pace for *tuans* to follow.

On the third day we laid up for two hours about noon and found a fresh water stream to bathe in. I took the hand-drawn maps out of the case and consulted the Dyak. He understood maps very well, as all primitives do, and pointed out our location immediately. We had covered the best part of thirty miles, which is damned good going in Malaya, believe me. If 'Flynn' and 'Tracy' had maintained a similar sort of pace over easier terrain then we would soon be converging on the fist-shaped area of the plantations. I wanted to reach the target zone in the early evening to allow us to keep watch from a high-ground position and be ready for a typical CT dawn attack. It goes without saying that I would have taken Shan on any terms, captive of any of the three groups, but that I wanted to kill or capture him myself. In three years in Malaya I had never come close.

Shan was as elusive as a will-o'-the-wisp. I had heard it said that he was possessed of magical powers and could fly on moonbeams and on the backs of gigantic owls. Settlement Chinese were terrified of him. Many families were intimidated into sending their sons to join his army, many more into providing food and shelter for the bandits. One would have assumed that a brutal murderer like Wei Sand Shan would have few allies. Surprisingly, however, there were converts and disciples scattered throughout the states. Four hundred and eleven murders had been laid at his door so far, including the deaths of thirty-six Europeans and twelve members of armed forces. Not a bad tally for an 'ally', what?

By the way, I never did receive an apology from the Select Committee of Inquiry who passed the judgement that my report on the shootings of Patterson, Prince and Landsdowne had been inaccurate and the result of 'delirium'. I am still mighty curious as to why the murders were hushed up. It hardly matters now. Shan flies under his true colours and is acknowledged as a bloody little murderer by all and sundry.

I suppose I should be grateful that I had Wei Sand Shan, my hatred of him and my burning desire to take revenge to sustain me while the dear old Japs were experimenting to see how much flesh they could strip from my bones without actually killing me and just how long a tapeworm they could cultivate in what was left of my gut – and all the rest of it. You know, I never hated the Japanese. I didn't even think of hating the Japanese. I was too busy hanging on to my will to live. At least, I consoled myself, I was going to be a participant in Shan's execution, and not just another footnote in the annals of the War Crimes Commission.

It did not occur to me, not even in my moments of rationality, that I would actually be able to hunt the swine myself, sporting the regimental badge and the old 'cherry beret', flanked by my trusty comrades of yore, Campbell and McNair.

Sometimes I considered it unfitting to harbour such homicidal urges, not proper for the son of a member of the English aristocracy or an officer in the SAS. But it is as it is. Shan himself adds fuel to the fire in my belly every so often. Indeed, if you had been with us when we came into the native village at Pentian, six track miles from the outer boundary of the three-thousand-acre Wade-Wingfield rubber plantation which itself lies twenty-two long miles from Port Kernan, you would surely have agreed.

The Wade-Wingfield tappers and their families were, of course, housed in protected *kampongs* close to the centre of the estate, virtually withing sight of the 'bungalow' in which the owner-manager – the Wade-Wingfield was privately owned – existed in a state of siege. One expected the Wade-Wingfield to be a target for the likes of Shan. It was inevitable that a 'defiant' plantation on the jungle's edge a devilish long way from town would attract the CTs like flies to a honeypot. But what motive the bandits had for massacre in the primitive hamlet at Pentian is beyond my ability to deduce. Was it no more than a delaying tactic?

It was a rough introduction to the methods of terrorists for Buz and McNair. Tough men though they were, even they found the sight that greeted us in that silent jungle clearing quite sickening and, by any sane law of war, totally without meaning. So much of what poses as a bid to possess the minds and hearts of a population seems to be meaningless, particularly to the victims. No rape, a little looting, selective slaughter. Selective? Lord, yes. Like some dark angel of the Old Testament, Wei Sand Shan had murdered the children.

How a man could do it, could deliberately put a bullet through the brain of a baby, is more than I can imagine. An infant, fat-limbed, healthy, loved; an infant too young to walk, let alone run away, lying on a raffia mat, shot with a .38 calibre bullet through the face. The infant might even have been chuckling as the muzzle of the gun came towards it, a split second before its soft little skull was blown apart.

Wei Sand Shan had not been *that* selective, of course. He had murdered some of the women too. Mothers of children who had obeyed blind instinct and had tried to stop the bandits doing their duty. Shan's men were not profligate with ammunition. Only a handful of the nineteen corpses had been shot. The others had been killed with knives – the wavy-bladed *kris* or axe-like *parang* or the razor-sharp tapping knife which the rubber workers used to draw latex from the trees. Who knows which piece of steel had done the work? Throats had been slit. Bellies had been slashed. Heads hacked off. It had been a deliberate series of actions. One could see a disciplined hand behind it, see Wei Sand Shan's glasses glinting with calculation as he pointed this way and that, picking the victims without cause.

There was a cause, of course. For men who live without gods, who make a god of a system, there has to be reason or there is nothing. The reason was simply that four of the young men of that paddi hamlet in the forest had refused to 'recruit' into Shan's army. It was not a noble decision, one made on point of principle, but rather one made out of fear. Fear backfiring on itself.

Somehow Shan had learned that the four young men, whose wives and children, sisters and brothers had the misfortune to live in that place, had gone to seek refuge in the Wade-Wingfield *kampong*. They had thus placed themselves beyond the pale, literally, as far as the Communist leader was concerned. Shan would not consider his afternoon's work as butchery, only as a just punishment, an object-lesson to Chinese who would not worship *his* gods, pagans who refused to bow to Marx, Lenin, Trotsky and Stalin and the new messiahs of freedom born in the mangers of China. To Shan these poor coolies had no political souls and were therefore less than human. One man, one gurgling infant, was nothing in the war of liberation.

'Oh, Christ!' said Buz Campbell, as soon as we made out the scene and our minds accepted what our eyes had taken in. The Canadian was not blaspheming. It was as if he fashioned a prayer to be delivered from such reality.

The Dyak stopped at the edge of the clearing. He would not go forward. He was a wise man, a sensible pagan. He knew that the dead as well as the living could do you irreparable harm.

Besides, the old men and women seemed to be conducting a ritual of their own, without, for once, a great mourning drama, a din of grief. Perhaps it was a rite of cleansing. Perhaps they were merely stunned.

The massacre had taken place only a couple of hours before we arrived. We couldn't have been more than three miles away, yet we had heard nothing, not even the muffled echo of a gunshot. The jungle had blanketed out every shriek and scream, absorbed the reverberations of the tragedy, kept it secret. Assassinate a colonel or a diplomat and the world shouts about anarchy and the need for control; murder peasants and there is hardly a murmur of protest in the marble halls of governing nations.

There was nothing we could do to help the Pentian survivors. Shan had left no wounded. Those he had intended to kill had been killed stone dead. Such is efficiency. All the children of the place up to the age of ten or eleven; a thread snapped, a generation wiped out: It was genocide in miniature. The community would probably not recover. I would send up a Red Cross team and a couple of chaps from the British Advisers' office whenever I could to persuade the remaining inhabitants that they would be better off in a compound. Traditionalists or not, I doubted if they would require much persuasion now.

Johnny took it upon himself to make the round of the little corpses, to ascertain that there was no life left. His soft walk, his gentle manner, seemed grieving, but being a Gurkha he was very tough. He picked out one old man – all knees and elbows – who was squatting by the doorway of one of the huts. The rest of us hung back. There was nothing we could do even if we had wished it, to comfort the poor folk. Vengeance was not on their minds; Malays are not like us.

Squatting too Johnny offered the old man tobacco which after hesitation the old man accepted. He had a scarred face. Yaws, I think, had chewed up his flesh. His nose was a cavity and his mouth was twisted. He pinched the cigarette between his fingers and smoked it in that manner. It was uncanny, the silence. One could hear the greedy drone of flies and not much else. After a few minutes of conversation Johnny returned to us and we gladly turned our backs on the scene and walked shakily to the spot where the Dyak waited.

Johnny said, 'It is Shan all right, Captain. Forty men, as far as I can make out the old fellow's arithmetic.'

Buz Campbell said, 'Why'd he butcher the kids?'

'Punishment.'

Johnny then explained what the old man had told him.

'Not one of the villagers understood what was going on. They supposed that it was food and only food the bandits had wanted. They brought their chickens and maize pots and their stocks of rice. Gave everything they had. The bandits made a meal which they ate while the children watched and the villagers cautiously got on with work to be done.'

I could vividly imagine the scene.

'Sand Shan got to his feet and told them they had been wicked. It had been arranged over tea-time, I think. The men, the Communists, had been instructed. It was no difficult task to catch children who had not the wit to run away.' Johnny shook his head. 'It took only a short time.'

'When did Shan leave?'

'The old man is not sure.'

'How far are we from the centre of the Wade-Wingfield?'

Johnny consulted the Dyak, using a mixture of tongues.

The Dyak spoke for himself. 'We retch night-time. Rightio. Genster Boss he ready go shootin' sun-comes-up. Far, fár us retch. But Umgah, he rightio tek in close.' He pointed. 'Wan, tew. Wan, tew. Me so.'

The Dyak knew only too well that Sand Shan would be in position for his dawn ambushes before we could reach the bungalow *kampong*. He was offering to lead us in after dark. It was a highly risky business. We might well give the game away if we stumbled across one of Shan's patrols. Shan was bound to have patrols out, to guard against the possibility of a flank or rear attack. I doubted if he would be expecting one, however. There probably wouldn't be more than a dozen CTs, in pairs or threes, in the bush fringe. But the closer we got to the bungalow (which together with the road to Port Kernan would be the focus of Shan's attacks) the more dangerous it would become.

The timing was haywire. I hadn't counted on Shan stopping off for this punitive exercise *en route*.

'Let's get the hell outta here,' Buz muttered.

The Canadian could not keep his gaze from the tumbled bundles in the grasses and on the beaten paths between the huts.

The dwellings were ragged, a shade too far from the plantation to have any sort of amenity, apart from a couple of galvanised buckets. There was no tin, no brick here. The houses were made of the fabric of thc jungle itself.

Why in God's name *had* Wei Sand Shan done it? I asked myself again.

One thing about British colonialists, they know when to leave well alone. In time we would have unrolled the trappings of control this far, would have brought medical aid, education and Coca Cola, but our corruption would have been benign and protective; at worst, overly bureaucratic. The madmen from Russia and the new China, heartless intellects like Wei Sand Shan, they brought nothing but their own icy lust for power at any price.

P.B. had his back to the village clearing. His jowls were bearded with a three-day growth, his eyes blazing blackly in the pinched face.

'Hey, Deke,' he growled, speaking in a low tone. 'How come everybody an' his bloody grandpa's out in the bloody open?'

I started to answer him without considering the implication of the question.

McNair's brows furrowed and he swivelled his eyes and gave an almost imperceptible jerk of the head.

Over his shoulder, as casually as possible, I scrutinised the square in front of the six houses.

It was true; the entire population of the village *was* out of doors, even very old women whom one would normally expect to be tucked out of the sun. The hideous circumstances had dulled my instinct. Fortunately P.B. had been more perceptive. The way in which the villagers were grouped, their passivity, caused me a dreadful qualm of recognition, reminding me of Java prison parades. I had been wrong, it was fright not ritual which kept the aborigines from removing the bodies for burial. No tribe that I had heard of would leave its dead to bloat in the sun and attract predators.

I licked my lips, which had gone dry as chalk. 'In which direction is the track to the rubber estate?'

The Dyak understood. He had sense enough not to point.

He said, 'Tween hearses.'

'Aye,' said P.B. 'Right between the houses.'

Buz stiffened. His hand moved slowly towards the Sten slung about his shoulder. For an instant it seemed as if Johnny would swing abruptly round.

I hissed out the order. 'Still. Stand absolutely still.'

P.B. said, 'Are you thinkin' what I'm thinkin', Deke?'

'Yes,' I said. 'It's a trap all right. It's a damned trap and we've walked right into it.'

P.B. gave a lopsided grin and made a strange, animal growl in his throat. 'Nearly, Deke,' he said. 'Nearly but not quite.'

3 Ambush alley

Sergeant Badhur was a regimental soldier. His family had had impeccable connections with the Gurkhas for fifty years. Great-grandfather Badhur had been on the march to Kandahar with Roberts, Father had fought at Festubert and Aubers and later at the Tigris in the First World War. He had left three of his brothers dead, one on each battleground. Sergeant Johnny Badhur had but one brother. They had served as boys together in the cadet squad at Dehra Dun then with the 2nd King Edward VII's Own Gurkhas, and had fought side by side against the Axis powers. When the time of 'the opt' came, in August 1947, Johnny's brother had elected to retire. Johnny had decided to 'opt' for service with the British not the Indian army. Consequently in March of 1948 he disembarked in Singapore with the bulk of the Gurkha regiment.

It was in the following year, during liaison patrols with the Malayan Police, that he encountered the 'mad major', Jeffrey Alexander Deacon, and struck up a friendship with the British ex-officer.

Johnny quickly learned Deacon's history and why the man was consumed with hunger for revenge. Over the months Johnny Badhur grew to respect Deacon's ability to check his impetuosity and play the long game – the only game worth playing in Malaya's hide-and-seek war.

Badhur's secondment to the Malayan Scouts (SAS) had been Deacon's doing. The transfer had given Johnny Badhur sleepless nights. Johnny was used to a life neatly pegged down by King's Regulations, morning parades and formal routine and he hadn't bargained for the cobbled-together nature of 'K' Squadron. He wasn't happy at Johore Sambong, nor did he approve of Deacon's rush into the jungle to back-door Wei Sand Shan with an untried unit.

Johnny still referred to the bandits by their self-designated ranks. He dignified them with a structure which, in essence, their companies did not possess. To Johnny Badhur, Shan's gang was No. 11 Company, Malayan (Independent) Communist Party. Reports that Wei Sand Shan was at loggerheads with central party officials and would have no truck with the Min Yuen underground network did not deter the Gurkha from regarding Sand Shan as a soldier. Deacon's methods seemed somehow unmilitary, almost cowardly. Shadowy doubts were personified when Deacon's henchmen turned up at Johore Sambong. They lasted during the training period and throughout the journey to the village of Petian. There they evaporated very swiftly.

From the moment the Scots corporal said, 'Nearly, but not quite', Johnny Badhur knew he was indeed in the company of true-blue fighters. Immediately, he felt more secure than he had done in weeks. It was so bloomin' obvious, he should have spotted it earlier. But he had been mesmerised by the sight of the poor little corpses and troubled by the realisation that Deacon had been right and he had been wrong. Sand Shan was no soldier: Sand Shan was nothing but a butcher-boy.

Without turning, Johnny Badhur waited to be told how they would free the village. He did not imagine that the three Britishers intended to slip away. There were bandits in hiding, bandits to be flushed out and killed. To Sergeant Badhur the odds mattered not a blessed bit. Odds could be levelled up by sensible soldiers with a clever strategy.

Captain Deacon said, 'Will the Dyak fight?'

Johnny wrapped his tongue around the pidgin Malayan. He saw by Umgah's reaction, a petulant underlip and glaring scowl, that the Dyak would indeed fight.

Deacon said, 'We daren't tarry, chaps. At any moment the bastards might suspect we've rumbled them and open fire.'

'How do we take them?' said Buz.

'Umgah will lead,' said Deacon. 'You and I, Buz, we'll come next. Johnny and P.B. in the rear. Do you see the avenue between the houses? It's my guess there are bandits hidden in the jungle along the trail. I think their intention is to wait until we're in the avenue then take us front and rear.'

'So we hit them short of the houses?' said Buz Campbell.

'Umgah will be vulnerable. Tell him that when I shout he must run for cover.'

Johnny conveyed the order.

The Dyak grunted. Already he was squinting about the square for suitable shelter.

Deacon said, 'Buz and I will drop where we are and immediately open fire.'

'What about the natives?' said P.B.

'Oh, they'll clear out at the first shot. They know the score.'

'Okay,' said P.B. 'You drop and shoot. Johnny an' me, we'll shove grenades in the windows.'

'That's it,' said Deacon.

'What of the contingent in the jungle?' asked Johnny Badhur, who was always thorough.

'We'll have to nail them too,' said Buz Campbell. 'Otherwise they'll horse back to Shan and blow the whole friggin' operation.'

'Johnny, Umgah an' me,' said P.B., 'we'll cut them off.'

'Fine,' Deacon agreed.

There was no need for further instruction. Good soldiers understood what had to be done and were tuned to do it without argument. To turn, to walk directly towards hidden enemy positions, took colossal confidence – but it was not foolish. It was the correct thing, the military thing, to do. Johnny Badhur approved.

'Now, Umgah,' said Deacon. 'Point to the track.'

With a sense of theatre that would have pleased Mr Gable himself, Umgah did so. He accompanied the gesture with a jabber of sound loud enough to be heard fifty yards across the compound.

During the two or three minutes of 'conversation', the villagers had not moved.

'Weapons ready. Not too obvious,' said Deacon. 'Off we go.'

Campbell and the Captain fell in ten or a dozen paces behind the Dyak, who with a weightless rolling gait had started in a straight line for the umber shadow of the avenue between the huts.

Grinning, McNair clapped a hand on Johnny's shoulder and made a fist gesture which would leave the bandits guessing. Under his breath the Scot said. 'I'm goin' t' get these dirty swine. Every last fuckin' one o' them.'

Johnny Badhur walked on aching feet, very lightly, muscles slack, ready for sudden activity. He speculated on what the Communists would be thinking. Were they suspicious? Nervous fingers on the triggers?

The entire SAS unit – all five of them – was exposed in the middle of the square. Natives squinted at them furtively, without lifting their heads, as if they were ashamed of their passivity.

In front of Johnny, Captain Deacon's bush shirt was black with sweat. Deacon held himself very upright, head high. The button over the canvas holster which held his Colt .45 automatic was undone. Cradled in his arms was a Sten. Buz Campbell's bulk blotted the house to the right from Johnny's view.

Campbell was truly a large man. He walked flat-footed, shambling like a bear. He carried a Sten at arm's length, seven pounds of metal in one hand, pistol-grip held lightly, foresight pointing to the ground. Johnny had a Sten too but he toted it in his left hand. Corporal McNair had an old-fashioned Mauser bolt-action rifle but it was the flapping grenade sack which counted. The canvas bag was clipped to the front of P.B.'s left hip. It contained ten 'Mills bombs', the old, tried-and-true defensive hand and rifle grenade which with modifications had been in service for thirty-five years. They remained quite lethal in effect.

Johnny had played much cricket in his boyhood and youth. He could throw a Mills a very long way, with accuracy. In his sack were six grenades. Four more were hooked on to his webbing belt beneath the skirt of his bush shirt. The heavy Bergens were a fearful encumbrance, though necessary to sustain the illusion that they were going innocently 'on their way' down the track.

The dark apertures of the house windows, empty of glass but protected by smooth 'blinds' of stained rattan, glowered at the Gurkha. He willed himself not to allow his gaze to dwell too long upon the windows. He counted his steps. Fifteen, sixteen, seventeen.

Beside him P. B. McNair stepped over the bare legs of a girl child of nine or ten years old who lay face down in the dust. Like him, Johnny noticed, the child had suffered from foot rot. Her heels were silvered with it. To the child it no longer mattered. Her discomfort was at an end.

Twenty-three, twenty-four, twenty-five.

Half-way across the compound.

By a quirk of the light, the wedge of jungle at the end of the avenue between the houses was tinted bright banana-leaf green. There was no sign of the CT Bren or Maxim which would be set up there, muzzle trailing their every step.

Twenty-seven, twenty-eight, twenty-nine.

Deacon shouted, '*Now!*'

The Captain pitched headlong to the dirt. The light astonished chatter of his Sten sounded before his belly hit the ground. Campbell faded from Johnny Badhur's view. The Gurkha was left exposed for a fraction of a second. Johnny had always considered himself fast but he was a tortoise compared to the Britishers and the big Canadian.

Two grenades were out of P.B.'s bag and in the air before Johnny could jerk the pin from the striker lever and feeling the lever snap in his fingers hurl the missile into the window of the hut to the left. He flung with a short whipping action but the sway of the Bergen on his back pulled the missile off line. It struck the woven wall of the house and dropped to the porch-like walk.

Johnny let the swing of the pack take him. He cut to his left out of range of fire of anything that might be in the jungle. McNair had already vanished. Johnny glimpsed the dot of another grenade in the air. He pitched on to his belly. On impact the shrug of the Bergen almost beheaded him. It loomed over his head, crushed his face into the dirt and caught the first three blast waves in rapid succession, whacking shocks into the Gurkha's skull. Ears singing, Johnny scrambled to his feet and ran then dropped to one knee, groped into the bag and, pulling himself together, armed and threw three grenades into the window spaces of the nearest hut.

P. B. McNair's instinct had been spot on. Spurts of gunfire from the huts confirmed it. Johnny almost forgot to fling himself down as the bamboo-framed palm-thatch hut rushed towards him in a disintegrating cloud which contained nothing solid apart from four timber posts. He could hear high-pitched wails, like gibbons in the morning, riding above the tornado roar. Splinters of bamboo and sheaves of twigs enveloped him along with hot dust and the acrid stink of the explosive. He was up and running again before the dust settled.

Veils of debris hung between him and the targets. The natives had scurried silently away, except for the old man, who had been struck in the back. He had tilted forward on to his knees like an ancient acrobat trying vainly to stand on his head. His long hands moved, groping very slowly at the ground like the legs of a poisoned crab. As Johnny went past, the old man toppled on to his side as if blown over by the wind of the Gurkha's passing.

Johnny was running hard now, oblivious to the *chek-chek-chek* of Jap-made submachine-guns, the whine of rifles. He aimed for the edge of the house and went round a gable of caked mud. A dog yapped and raced away under the dwelling. Snapping the straps and dipping out from under it, Johnny shed the Bergen. He felt more like a soldier now and uttered a low guttural cry as he ran forward to the corner of the native house.

There was a stand of withered maize, hardly worthy of being called a crop, and two long strings upon which hung garments. A decaying bullock-cart, turned over on its side, tilted its broken wheels skywards. A yellowish-brown *merawan* tree of no great height dominated the fern clumps and jungle croppings. A boy, naked except for a loincloth, squatted by the tree.

In Malayan, Johnny Badhur asked, 'Are they there?'

The boy, eight or nine years old, nodded and pointed around the tree into the jungle on a line with the line of the track.

'How many?' asked the Gurkha.

Counting was part of the most primitive schooling, thank God. The boy made a crest with two fingers of each hand.

Johnny Badhur sucked in breath, ducked around the gable, ran to the boy and flung himself against the protection of the *merawan*. He looked down at the child, who stared up at him with black expressionless eyes.

'Do they have a big gun?'

The child nodded again.

Johnny smiled and as if for luck touched his fingertips fleetingly upon the sleek, black hair. He slid round the *merawan* tree and lifting up his feet with care picked his way into the jungle.

Smoke, thin and flameless, hovered over the houses. Though there were still sporadic shots, the firing sounded cautious now. Before the leaves closed behind him Johnny saw a group of natives hidden behind an ox-tether in the lee of a low mud wall. Some had their faces in their hands, others had palms clapped to their ears. Behind them the rear wall of one house had been blown flat, its weave intact. He wondered where the Dyak had got to and if Captain Deacon and the Canadian had escaped unscathed from the compound.

The undergrowth was scant. Leaves trembled in the afternoon light, stirred by an indistinct breeze. Thirty yards or so into the trees Johnny traversed the edge of the village.

Though only minutes had passed since Captain Deacon had ordered the attack, the bandits who manned the machine-gun on the trail might have abandoned it and started after the main guerrilla body. Why had Shan left a detail behind? Had he known that he was being tracked by an SAS unit? Had he somehow managed to make contact with his spies at Port Kernan? If so there would be more trouble ahead. The onus would have shifted; Shan would have surprise on *his* side.

Breathing through his nose, the Sten held across his chest, the Gurkha shouldered through the vegetation.

Johnny heard them before he saw them. They had stopped firing the machine-gun and were arguing, in a Chinese dialect which he could not interpret, over it. There were four of them. He could tell by their confusion that they were the sort of peasants who could not operate without forceful leadership. He lifted a spray of fern with the muzzle of the Sten and viewed them clearly. Boys of not more than nineteen or twenty, smart enough in the polyglot uniform of the so-called Communist Army, but more like children playing a game than real soldiers. They seemed to be arguing as to whether they should take the machine-gun or leave it. Should they go back into the village? Why had nobody told them what was going on? The Gurkha recalled the alacrity with which the SAS group had made its decisions and formulated its plans. If this was the quality of Wei Sand Shan's terrorists then the half-war would not last long after all, certainly not in this province.

Johnny hoisted up his Sten. He had no chance to fire it, however.

Four shots sounded like one, a whistle of rapid fire. One of the Chinese whirled, spun round by the impact of a bullet penetrating his skull. The others did not even have time to flinch. They fell where they stood, almost simultaneously. One slumped across the machine-gun which canted on its tripod and crashed under him.

Crouching, Johnny Badhur called out, 'Corporal McNair?'

'Aye.'

'If you cover me,' said the Gurkha, 'I will make sure they are quite dead.'

'They're dead okay,' said McNair. 'But on y'go. I've got the trail in my sights.'

Cautiously Johnny went forward. With the Sten in his right hand, he turned each of the bandits over. Each had been drilled through the head by a single bullet. Blood and brain-matter matted their hair or ran like candle-wax down the faces of the dead terrorists. From nowhere flies appeared.

'Told you,' said McNair.

Johnny looked round. He still could not see the Scot.

'Where are you?'

'Over here.'

'I think it is safe to come out.'

P. B. McNair emerged from cover on the far side of the trail. He had fired from an upright stance, using a tree bole as a brace for his shoulder. He seemed pleased by his thirty seconds' work.

Grinning, he said, 'Well, I have nae lost the touch.'

Johnny said grimly, 'It is very fine shooting, Pete. You were a sniper in the war?'

'Aye, right.'

Johnny looked down the main trail. It was broader than he had anticipated, earth tamped down, grass and weeds cut back, broad enough for two men to pass along it side by side.

'Did you see if four men were all?' Johnny asked.

McNair said, 'Only four when I got here. Maybe there was more but it doesn't seem very likely.'

The Scot, on his knees, examined the guerrillas' arms.

The machine-gun was a variation of the old No. 92 Taisho, with a right-side cocking mechanism and an optical sight. It had been modified to take rimless 7.7mm cartridges fed from linked strips, had a tripod mount and removable barrel of wormscrew design. Mechanism and tripod tubes were in good condition, with no sign of rusting. In fact the weapon, though six or seven years old, seemed factory-fresh. It had, however, jammed.

P. B. McNair's fingers expertly tinkered with the breech. 'Got an extraction fault. Grit in the lubrication pad.'

'For us it is as well perhaps that the gun jammed.'

'Och, no.' McNair got to his feet. 'They couldn't see what they was firin' at. What kind of woodchopper is this, anyhow?'

Johnny told him it was Japanese and gave him a potted history of the type. He concluded, 'The CTs, they have many such arms hidden in the jungle.'

'I hope they're all like this one,' said McNair, kicking the weapon. 'Anyway, maybe we should take a wee toddle down the track.'

'Should we not first check with the Captain?'

'He'll be okay,' said McNair. 'C'mon, man. We're supposed t'make sure nobody gets away.'

Johnny glanced through the leaves at the narrow view of the village. More smoke and pale flames licked up from the thatched roofs but the sound of firing had ceased.

'As you wish,' he said.

Neither the Gurkha nor the Scot were trained trackers. But the path from the village was well used. It would have been difficult for anyone to pick up clues to indicate that a pair of bandits had dropped back from the machine-gun crew and lay in wait a quarter of a mile away at the point where the main path diverged into seperate jungle trails.

Seeing nothing, hearing nothing, the Gurkha and the Scot had relaxed their vigilance by the time they reached the division.

They stopped at the Y-shaped crossroad.

Johnny pointed to the left fork. 'It will be this one to the Wade-Wingfield we will take.'

'Is yon the way Sand Shan went?'

'I suspect so.'

'Well,' said P. B. McNair, 'there's nothin' here an' no sign anybody's come along it in a hurry.'

'I agree. We will go back.'

As they turned, the grenade came hurtling out of the tree-stand at the junction of the fork. They saw no movement only the tiny anomalous black object in motion against the vegetation. It had been thrown badly, out of a cramped position perhaps and on too flat a trajectory. For a split second Johnny thought that McNair had gone crazy.

The Corporal leapt upon him in a flying tackle, lifted the Gurkha and rammed them both into the undergrowth to the left of the trail. Even as they hit the dirt, McNair pressed Johnny's face into the ground and covered him with his body.

The grenade exploded on the track.

Dirt rained down upon the soldiers. The blast wave shook through them. Fragments of the missile hissed and *thocked* around their legs and thighs.

'Bloody bleedin' hell!' McNair cried.

He rolled away from the Gurkha, groping in the undergrowth for the Mauser he had dropped in his haste.

The guerrillas' crossfire was lethal. It seemed as if there was a whole damned army sunk behind the trees. Johnny had been through this sort of experience before. He realised that the sting had gone out of the attack. Because of the failure of the first grenade to kill or maim, the thrust had been levelled out. Not that he and McNair were out of trouble but they had cover and in the jungle cover was all important.

The chatter of automatic weapons didn't trouble the Gurkha so much as his own carelessness. If it hadn't been for McNair's speed of reaction he would be a dead man now, and nobody but himself to blame. Cursing, Johnny rolled over and snake-crawled away from the track.

Leaves were flapping and flicking with the spray of bullets but he knew that he could not be seen. The guerrillas had not thought to put a man in a tree. Perhaps they had not had time. He did not attempt to look behind him or to draw McNair in his wake. Elbows and knees working like paddles, he crawled quickly and expertly, relieved that he wasn't still wearing the Bergen which would have made him as obvious as an elephant in this humiliating situation.

The first intensive barrage had eased, though the guerrillas were still firing. The ambushers would be reloading or more probably changing positions. Paddle-crawling, he kept down and wondered what McNair had done with himself.

The thing happened so very, very quickly, Johnny had time only to cry out. He knew it was a bandit the moment the knee thumped into his back, pinning him to the ground. He felt a forearm wrap around his forehead, cotton hat sliding off. His head was jerked back. Out of the corner of his eye he saw the glint of a tapping knife, the blade which would slice through his windpipe and jugular vein. He would die within seconds, drowning in his own blood.

He rammed his forehead to the ground and thrust the Sten up in both hands to protect the nape of his neck. But a stab was inevitable, somewhere along the spine, a blow which would sap him and let the bandit's long knife find his throat. Johnny Badhur knew that he was finished. At most, he had thirty seconds to live.

The attacker's wrist struck the braced Sten, missing his neck. The fellow jumped and wriggled, straddling him. Fierce wrenching pressure clamped his head, back-breaking, neck-cracking pressure which Johnny could no longer resist. He waited for the slippery kiss of the razor-sharp blade on his exposed throat.

Then it was gone, pressure and weight. The tapping knife hit the earth by his face. He flinched from it, twisting like a salmon on a spear, as if in fear that the weapon might possess an energy of its own, might slit his windpipe still.

Johnny pitched the Sten out ahead of him and rolled. He got his knees under him and swung into a sitting position. He reached for the dagger he kept tabbed to his webbing belt. He had no need of it. The Dyak had done the job for him. The Dyak's features were grotesquely joyful, dark skin darkened by effort, eyes bulging, red mouth gaping with mute laughter.

The long-bladed *parang* was used with an economy which reminded Badhur of the fish quays of Madras – ripping, chopping, resistance of bone and gristle, the swollen muscles of the Dyak's arms. The Communist's head parted from his shoulders, neck sawn through. Pendants of bloody tissue and white sinew hung from the collar of flesh. Pushed to one side, the body bubbled blood as lungs emptied through torn tubes. Smooth, thin, yellow-tinted legs kicked and thrashed. Rubber-soled boots danced a final hideous jig as the Dyak thrust the carcass away and, on his knees, held the head up to be admired.

The guerrilla still wore his hat.

Though mighty glad to be alive, Johnny felt his gut heave and, on all fours, threw up his breakfast, while the Dyak, champing with delight, twirled the bloody head this way and that.

A scream reached out of the undergrowth on the tail of a burst of rifle-fire. There was a crashing noise and another grenade exploded. Johnny did not feel threatened. He was still vomiting.

Instinct told him that the SAS veteran was mopping up the bandits, to make amends perhaps for having cocked up in the first place.

Deacon to Holms: August 1951

Buz and I had already set off down the trail when the sounds of the attack reached us. Naturally, I had to restrain Buz. Worried about his chum McNair, he would have gone charging ahead. The ruse at the village had worked beautifully. We caught the bandits by surprise and gained the few seconds vital to success. Native houses offer little protection against grenades and high-powered bullets. The CTs were well and truly trapped. Besides, they had made a tactical error by occupying only the dwellings which directly flanked the track. It would have been more sensible to lie off the fire-line or to put snipers in the trees. I suspect that Wei Sand Shan left them behind only as a precaution, not because he knew for sure that Special Force units were on his trail. It did occur to me, I confess, that 'Tracy' and 'Flynn' might have been inadvertently spotted. They were each a valley away but Shan had an excellent 'wire service' of native runners. Whatever the reason, Shan had elected to leave an ambush party of twelve men. He had not picked his most seasoned troops for the detail.

Disappointingly, we took none alive. It was unfortunate, and not intentional, that all were killed. I could have used a terrified prisoner or two to yield information on Shan's strength and disposition and his precise destination. How would I have obtained the information? Would I have ignored the code of the regiment, the 'rules' of war? Not exactly. I would have threatened to turn them over to the Dyak.

Inspection of the arms carried by the CTs showed the usual thing – Japanese weapons, quite new, modified to take available ammunition. Even the grenades were of Japanese manufacture. As I already knew, Shan was independent of the normal sources of supply for arms and ammunition, a fact which gave him much of his power as a guerrilla. No clapped-out, patched-up rubbish for his troops. No rusty American Thompsons or British Enfields.

We had no opportunity to turn out the personal possessions from the pockets of the corpses. Buz was agitated. He wanted to go at once to check on McNair and Johnny Badhur, in spite of my assurances that Johnny knew what he was doing. I gave in, however, and we were fairly hot on the heels of the Indian and the Scot when the firing started.

By the time we got there, it was all over.

It was a grisly sight, worse by far than the head-shot corpses by the machine-gun at the top of the trail. Though used to gore and the less savoury sights of jungle warfare, Johnny had been shaken by the experience. His complexion was the tint of a Sten barrel, his eyes huge. He had been sick and had not had time to clean himself properly. He muttered apologies while McNair, cool as ever, sat by the fork in the trail with two dead bandits laid out like trout by his side.

The Scot smoked a cigarette and seemed not at all put out by the Dyak, who was carefully wrapping a human head in banana leaves preparatory to stowing it into a haversack. The Dyak too was smoking a cigarette which pointed straight out from his mouth and jerked this way and that as he chatted contentedly to his trophy, telling it what a brave warrior it had belonged to and how he would be a worthy keeper of its spirit.

Now I would not want you to think that such behaviour is the norm. Rough and ready our squadrons may be, most unlike the disciplined SAS units you commanded, but we haven't sunk, in general, to the depths of depravity. I put up with the Dyak because he was an astonishing fighter and a tracker of almost supernatural powers. I don't say that I took to him personally.

Convinced that we had prevented any of the bandits from making an escape, and hopeful that Wei Sand Shan had left no more rearguard details further down the track, we returned to the village at the double, leaving the Dyak and McNair to haul the bodies out of sight of the trail.

Johnny Badhur had calmed himself. He was able to tell me what had happened. He blamed himself; the truth was that he had been careless. McNair was a novice to guerrilla methods and might have been excused for not being on his toes. Johnny, however, had slipped up. The fact that it had almost cost him his life was punishment enough. I could not determine which aspect of the ambush had undermined his nerve. Was it almost having his throat slit or was it his close-hand witness of the Dyak's blood ritual?

As soon as we reached the village and saw that the natives had come out of hiding and were gathering themselves together for the sad task of burying their dead with due ceremonies, I decided that we must move on without delay.

I instructed Badhur to fill the water bottles from the clean-water cisterns and to make us a brew of tea. We were all thoroughly dried out by the feverish activity of the last half-hour.

The headman of the village, a grizzled elder, thanked us for what we had done. It was a formal and monotonous harangue and consumed time, but I did not have the heart to be brusque with him. Meanwhile Buz got on with the business of searching the dead. He placed their personal items on a raffia mat, and when the headman had finished his speech I sifted through the stuff, separated the photographs (the usual sort of snaps) and three letters and put them safe in my pocket. It is from such unpromising sources that Special Branch obtains its leads. Identifying bandits is half the battle and one never knows for sure what clues might be contained in letters.

McNair and Umgah joined us. The Dyak had left his trophy in its sack, the sack hung from a branch by the mouth of the trail.

Johnny had fallen quiet now. He drank a great deal of tea, laden with sugar which we scrounged from the villagers, but ate none of the biscuits which I broke from the rations. P.B., on the other hand, was rather pleased with himself. He recounted the action blow by blow for the edification of Campbell.

In an hour or less it would be dark. We were still many miles from the centre of the Wade-Wingfield rubber plantation. Weary though we were, it would be necessary to make a trek through the pitch-black jungle. Fortunately the trail was wide and Umgah confident that we would reach the rubber by five o'clock a.m.

As we quit the compound, we passed a couple of Communist posters which one of Shan's more ardent villians had spiked to the wall of a house. In the heat of the action, none of us had noticed them before.

One said, DESTROY THOSE WHO ROB LABOUR BY UNDER-PAYING MEN.

Would the chubby native baby shot through the head have appreciated the injunction and considered the exchange of sunlight and warm milk worth it?

The other said, DESTROY ALL THOSE WHO WORK FOR OTHER RACES.

The wayside pulpit of political gangsters had ironic overtones.

Umgah toted his haversack across his shoulder and carried his spears, crossed, in his right hand. Behind him came the

Indian, limping a little, then a Canadian, a Scot and me, son of a landed English gentleman – all of us, even the Dyak, far, far from home.

Allison Wingfield's brother, Jack Greville-Wheeler, farmed land not far from my family's seat in Shropshire. He had ridden in the Brooke Hunt with my father. I was told this startling fact by Clive Wingfield shortly after our first meeting, at a dinner-dance in the Academy in Port Kernan. It was one of the few social events which I felt absolutely obligated to attend. The invitation had come from Malaya's number-one copper. I was to escort his younger daughter, who was 'visiting Papa' from England. Apparently I was chosen for this singular honour because of my sobriety. Perhaps Colonel Augustus Saunders also believed the ugly rumour (my medical records notwithstanding) that I had been castrated by the Japanese. For whatever reason, I was the one who was saddled with the obnoxious little creature. Sober or drunk, and with my appendages intact, there was never the slightest danger of my animalistic urges being aroused by Saunders' rosy little chatterbox.

Allison Wingfield was quite another story. There was more to Mrs Wingfield than met the eye. What met the eye was by no means inconsiderable. Allison conformed to the *mores* of respectable society by not 'throwing it around', however. The truth is that she didn't have to. She was the dream girl of every bachelor in the state, the idol of most of the married men too. She was truly beautiful, dark and active and, when I first met her, just a little on the plump side, like a Rubens' Venus. She was also a crack shot and hated the Communists with unbridled ferocity. She was a tall woman, in contrast to her husband. Clive was a tiny little bantam of a man, ten or twelve years Allison's senior.

Wingfield was cocky and sly, with the glaucous eyes of one who drinks too much. He was suspicious of everyone – planters, policemen, tin-miners, engineers, diplomats and soldiers. Especially soldiers. Not without justification Clive assumed that every male he met was intent on making him a cuckold. To the best of my knowledge Allison Wingfield had given her husband no cause to doubt her loyalty. But her vitality and her friendliness must have seemed to Clive like an open invitation to adulterers.

Although he boasted to me of his wife's family 'connections', he didn't trust me either. When I turned up on the estate a couple of weeks after the Academy dinner-dance, the fact that I was accompanied by a dozen armed soldiers didn't seem to temper his doubts. He showed me his defence arrangements with ill will, doled out 'hospitality' grudgingly and in general gave me short shrift. I began to believe the talk in town, to subscribe to the theory that Clive Wingfield was on his way to becoming a loony.

Many planters were pretty eccentric, as if they were trying to live like characters in a Somerset Maugham novel. They drank too much. Scandals were not uncommon. In a society which had more than its share of recluses and hermits, Wingfield took the biscuit.

The Wade-Wingfield's acres were defended by jungle and swamp. The roads were not in good repair. Clive refused point-blank to have anything to do with 'caring and sharing' committees which had been formed to give strength and succour to outlying plantations. He ran the rubber side of it well enough, took a good tonnage and was generous to his tappers and their families. But he wanted no truck with his peers. He was proud of his wife, insanely jealous of her and – I think – not too unhappy that the terrorists had added another line of defence to his remote and inhospitable fortress.

When I picked the targets for 'Gable', 'Tracy' and 'Flynn', I chose Wingfield's place for myself for the simple reason that I wanted to see the woman again. That wasn't the only reason, of course. The Wade-Wingfield had been under attack almost constantly since the beginning of the year when Shan's groups moved into the sector. Clive Wingfield was a fighter, that I will say for him.

The bungalow was almost impregnable and Wingfield had armoured his Land Rover with steel plates and other paraphernalia cut from old wartime tanks, a graveyard of which lay in an adjacent valley. He had so much armour on the Land Rover that it could barely crawl along at a top speed of thirty mph, but it would have taken a howitzer shell to penetrate its cabin. He had shaped a tight compound. He had installed arc lights and howler sirens, operating from separate generators. Going the whole hog, Wingfield had even built a tower of sorts into the roof of the bungalow and had dug up a damned Lewis gun, the type that used to be supplied to coastal boats for anti-aircraft protection. Where he had found the ammunition is beyond my guess but there are places in Singapore where you can shop for such esoteric items if you are willing to pay the price.

One of the jokes going the round in Port Kernan was that the Lewis gun was Clive Wingfield's chastity belt. It was said that the houseboys were employed not to keep the CTs from slaughtering tappers or blowing up transport trucks but to keep Allison safe from ruttish planters who would stop at nothing to possess her fair body.

Why do I spare so much space for this trivial gossip? Because it is relative. Clive Wingfield's paranoid fancies led to other things. They were no more to be sneered at than the patriotic exhibitions which flourished in those early months of the Emergency, in flag-raising ceremonies conducted on barbed-wire verandahs by bugle-playing managers and sixgun-toting directors. It was great sport – and if you don't believe me, perhaps you will take me more seriously when I tell you that the chaps in the Port Kernan tennis club, who met every Sunday prompt at noon for a set or two of doubles and many *stengahs*, ran a book on which of them would be raided next and which of them would be next to die.

It was to this that we came, crawling through pitch-black jungle, to 'rescue' Clive Wingfield and his beautiful wife from a raid of such magnitude that not even the Lewis gun on the roof would serve as protection.

Sand Shan had no interest in the Wingfields' domestic nexus or in the planter's foibles. Sand Shan intended to raze the estate to the ground purely to demonstrate the might of the Communist Party and to enhance his reputation as number-one rebel, a terrorists' terrorist. To the best of my knowledge the Chinese bandit had never clapped eyes on Allison Wingfield.

Wingfield had cleared out dry rubber trees all around the

bungalow and had planted new ones which were stripling-small and gave no cover. Therefore the bungalow sat in a wide clearing and was difficult to attack. Workers' quarters, the usual shacks, ran in two straight lines to the east of the bungalow and the lot, including smokehouses, and drying racks for latex, generators, truck sheds etc. were all contained within a high fence of barbed wire.

The boundary of the plantation was partly fenced and patrolled. On the gate Wingfield posted a three-man guard night and day; armed Tamils, not the best soldiers in the world but loyal enough and not stupid. There were nine Tamils in all. Wingfield paid them well and allocated them the best quarters. When he made his morning round in the Land Rover, Clive Wingfield was accompanied by an armed Malay overseer who had worked on the estate for many years and whom he had inherited from his original partner, now deceased. The venerable (and venerated) Mortimer Wade was, I gather, a free-wheeling old reprobate. While Clive was out on his rounds, Allison manned the Lewis gun in the tower. The Wingfields were not going to be caught napping.

All of this Sand Shan would be sure to know. He would also know that the Wingfields had 'accounted for' eleven CTs dead and about twenty seriously wounded, and that so far the weekly run of rubber to Port Kernan had not been stopped by bandit raids. Clive Wingfield was shrewd enough to change his schedule every week. Though the CTs were patient hunters, Clive's ingenuity in getting his crop to town must have annoyed the Red leader very much.

Jungle travel in the heart of the night made me nervous. It is all too easy to become paranoid in strangling vegetation, accompanied by the weird hobgoblin noises of nocturnal creatures, including a wakeful tribe of monkeys which seemed intent on following us all the way to the rubber trees.

We walked in single file, Umgah in the lead. We held a rope in our left hands, keeping it tight, like so many wooden ducks on a string. Thanks to the Dyak's skill, however, we made excellent time along the trail.

I was dogged by the notion that Shan might have left another ambush party behind or rigged booby-traps – a staked pit is particularly nasty – but as the miles dropped behind us and we came close to the rubber my fears on that score dwindled.

By now, as you may imagine, we were all feeling the strain. My legs were trembling and my pack felt like a ton weight upon my back, the Sten as heavy as a damned field-gun. In front of me on the rope was Johnny Badhur, limping with the pain in his diseased feet. Campbell and McNair seemed game enough. McNair's only grumble was that I would not let him smoke.

Latex, as you may know, runs best in the very early morning. It had been custom for the director/owners of rubber plantations to make rounds before dawn, for the tapping to begin before the sun came up. Dangers inherent in touring the trees in semi-darkness, however, had pushed the start-time back by an hour. Clive Wingfield would not rouse his workers until six a.m. I had the feeling that Sand Shan would adhere to the classic method of attack and hit the central compound a half-hour after first light, catching the *tuan* and the *mem* separate and apart, and the workers scattered.

Life in the jungle took its eternal course. One orchestra retired and another took its place; then there was that peculiar interlude of damp silence which preceded the 'hour of birth and death', as the Hokkien Chinese call it. When we gathered for our last breather, we could hear our bodies functioning – pulse, heart-beat, abdomen and lungs – and every sound seemed as loud as a thump on a *rabana* drum. We were near to the rubber now, coming down into the hind part of the Wade-Wingfield, a belt of low scrub and grassland which in Wade's golden days had provided farm and grazing belts for his liberated workers. Scorched and tilled and scorched again, the jungle had never quite reclaimed the strip. In 1946 and '47, before the Emergency, Clive and Allison Wingfield had shot game here and had been, I suppose, happy enough in their way.

Softly now, groping out each step, we proceeded without the guide string out of the skirt of the jungle and in line abreast crossed the *pampas* hem into the dark arches of Clive Wingfield's rubber trees. If my guess was right we had less than half an hour to find positions and if possible locate the bandits before the shooting started. For once, I wasn't thinking of Wei Sand Shan.

In my mind's eye I saw Allison Wingfield in her netted bed, rising sleepily as the alarm rang, night-gown discarded as she padded towards the shower, desirable, vulnerable and in grave danger, like a lady in a dark castle in King Arthur's time. Did it ever happen to you, Colonel? Were you ever suddenly and unexpectedly freed from fighting out of hatred or for hazy principles? As I crept down the pillared avenue of rubber trees that morning, I felt more cheerful than I had done in years, since the treacherous ju-ju man had traded me to the Japanese, in fact.

At last, at last, I was spoiling for a fight!

Ridiculous as it may sound, I needed Allison Wingfield to erase the images of butchered children and honest soldiers shot in the back. I had no idea, of course, that it would turn out as it did.

Umgah touched my arm and drew me down behind the bole of a rubber tree. I could smell that odd, indescribable odour which the sealed slits in the bark give off. The ground was sticky under my knees where little oozing droplets of sap had trickled from the cups of the previous day's tappings and the quiet bare feet of natives had trodden it into the grass.

The Dyak pointed.

Through shrouded trunks I saw the cold mist of the morning backlit by Wingfield's arc-lamps and, peering, the gable wall of the bungalow. Even as we watched, a light appeared in the gable's only window, adding warmth and dimension to the scene.

Once more the Dyak touched my arm.

The bandits were before us, backs to us, a dozen or more strung out among the trees. My elation increased. My plan was going to work. 'Gable' would bring 'em in, dead or alive.

Signalling, I led the boys forward towards the bungalow, moving like shadows among the rubber trees, guided by the light behind which the Wingfields made ready for another day.

Allison Wingfield fitted the 38c-cups of the cotton brassière over her breasts and struggled with the stiff new eye-hooks on the back of the strap. Even that slight exertion brought a dew of perspiration to her skin and the refreshing moments after the shower became a pleasure forgotten.

Today would be hot, hotter than yesterday. If the rain that Tavvi, the senior houseboy, predicted did fall in the early afternoon, tonight would be insufferably muggy and Clive would drink himself into a morose stupor once more.

She stood with her back to the mirror and fiddled with the catch, then impatiently she padded into her husband's bedroom.

'Do me up, please, Clive.'

Clive Wingfield was seated on the end of the narrow wooden bed. The mosquito net was slung back and the metal-shaded lamp on the table angled to give him a focus of light. He wore only the undershorts he had slept in, and his jowls were grizzled with a day's growth of beard. A cigarette dangled from his lips and, stooped over the old blue-steel Colt .45 automatic which lay reverently on a towel on his knees, he looked, Allison thought, like an ancient Semais, not one of the men but one of the women. His matted hair and the wrinkled unrevealing eyes increased the likeness, but the ugly Colt was an anomaly, for the Semai peoples were harmless and non-violent and that was not something one could say about her husband.

'Clive?'

The man grunted and squinted up at her.

She had put on plain cotton briefs and her hair was still moist, but her husband gave her less attention than he would have given one of the tappers in the compound below the house. There was no greeting, no good-morning kiss. His fingers did not touch her flesh as he fumblingly clipped the hooks together. Instantly he returned his attention to the gun.

God knew, the Colt needed no attention. It had not been fired in a fortnight and had been cleaned, stripped and cleaned eight or nine times. The Colt was only one of the many fetishes that Clive had adopted in a year of decline. A matched pair of Vaughan shotguns was another. They shared Clive's monastic bedroom and in three or four minutes' time, after he had emptied and reloaded the Colt's magazine, he would take each of the shotguns down and wipe its parts with a chamois cloth.

On a beaded linen coaster on the night-table stood a tall glass of whisky and lime juice which Bert, the second houseboy, brought in every morning and with which Clive would 'rinse out' his mouth.

Standing close by, Allison could smell the sour sweat from his body mingled with the sharpness of the whisky and the oiled metal of the Colt. She watched him in sorrow as he thumbed the cartridges into the lips of the magazine. He heeled the magazine into the slot in the butt and laying the piece on the towel reached for his whisky sour. A cigarette pinched in finger and thumb, he drank and swallowed, replaced the cigarette in his mouth and the glass on the table and got on with the ritual of polishing the gun.

Allison hurried back into her bedroom before irritation could mount into anger. Such reactions left her husband confused and uncertain, and he had more than enough on his mind.

She dressed in a fresh cream-coloured pants suit and diligently belted on the silly red leather holster which Clive had given her last Christmas. From under her pillow she took the Bulldog, a solid-frame pocket revolver, and tucked it in the holster.

'Never,' Clive had told her, 'be parted from that little beauty. A Bulldog can bring down a man at twenty paces. It isn't every planter's wife who has her own "comforter", you know.'

There were dashed few 'ornamental' wives in Malaya these days; the pretty, feather-headed girls had all packed up and headed for home. Sometimes she wished she had gone with them. But it was not in her to turn tail, to be less than loyal to her poor neurotic husband. Guns did not frighten her – she had grown up with them – but the effect of the disintegration of law and order, of structured society, upon Clive did: she worried more for his sanity than for his life.

Clive did not hate the CTs as other planters did. His defiance was mulish in the extreme. He did not hope to 'win', but merely not to be defeated. Deep in her heart, a secret even to herself, Allison Wingfield felt that it was too late. Clive had been defeated not so much by the bandits as by life itself. So great was his compulsion to deny the CTs their will that he had come to deny everything.

The Wade-Wingfield was more than their home. It was their investment for the future. The property had dropped in value, of course, since the war began but it still turned a decent profit, provided Clive could keep it in production. Rubber prices were climbing. The clearing-houses for latex in KL and Singapore could not get enough of the stuff. On that short-term score Clive had nothing to worry about. But worry he did. A dry, unshared fretting had worn down his nerves and undermined their marriage. For a man like Clive, no longer in the flush of youth, it was hell being a 'true Brit' under pressure.

For the Wingfields the day did not begin with ceremonies of defiance. There were no flag-raising, no blowing of bugles, no inspection of the workers or parade of the household staff. Clive's ceremonies were conducted in private, with the guns and the whisky sour, as he screwed up his courage to go outside and make his morning tour, desperately afraid of what might happen to him and to his plantation.

Allison's contribution to the morning ritual was to ascend from her bedroom on the house's second level and climb the wooden staircase from the old verandah to the watch-tower which jutted incongruously through the red tile roof. Fort Zinderneuf, Clive called it, borrowing inappropriately from *Beau Geste*. Though he had shown Allison how to load and operate the Lewis gun, the purpose of her early-morning visit to the stubby little tower was to act as scout. Her job was to scan the acres of rubber and the swollen crests of the jungle, to inspect, through high-magnification Zeiss binoculars, the visible section of the road to Port Kernan and the compound beneath the arc-lamps. She did this on her knees, head down, moving from aperture to aperture on each side of the square tower.

The tappers were already up and about and sight of her movements was a signal for the first shift to move towards the assembly point from which they would be trucked to the 'open' section. They carried their razor-sharp knives and cups and the tin buckets in which the thickening sap would be collected. As a group they looked picturesque and colourful. At the doorways of the huts, women were already busy with brooms, and bedding had been brought out to air. Though fireplaces and stoves were installed, some of the villagers preferred to cook in the open air. The flicker of small fires, safe in little concrete hearths, brightened the grey dawn gloom.

At the three water taps in the front of the huts children gathered, lugging buckets, to draw the day's supply. Across the compound, across the remnants of the *tuan*'s flower garden, the chirpy sounds of Malay voices came to her. Indians, Malays, Chinese – it made no matter. If there was an attack, large or small, that day or any other, the workers would not lift a finger to assist in their own defence. They were 'looked after' and protected and remained child-like in their response to the bandits' barbarity. Fearful, they did nothing, put up no resistance, would not retaliate.

Allison trailed the binocular lenses across the workers' lines. The air was vibrant with the hum of insects. A hornbill craked loudly in the trees behind the house. Generators purred steadily. She could even hear the thin whirring hiss that the arc-lamps gave off in the moist air.

Below the trap, at the foot of the short staircase, Clive's boots thudded.

'All clear?' he shouted.

'Wait.'

Allison focused on the road, searching out of habit for some unusual shape in the fringe growth, for some object that should not have been there. She saw nothing. She switched to the uniform ranks of rubber trees which stretched out west of the compound and peered at full magnification up each of the breathless aisles. Nothing.

'All clear.'

'I'm going down now.'

'All right.'

Once, she would have told him, 'Take care, dear', but no longer. She knew that he would take care – excessive, obsessive care. She could not be sure of her feelings, could not gauge the extent of the changes in her attitude to her husband. She was beginning to suspect that Clive was at heart a coward.

In an hour he would return and they would breakfast together. In the interim he expected her to man the Lewis gun as if she was part of an elaborate, almost religious, charm which he had woven to protect himself. If there was trouble, and there often was, he would cope with it. But the day would come, soon perhaps, when he would not cope with it, and she would be left in the ridiculous tower, surrounded by nothingness, at the mercy of the bandits. If Clive did not come back from the outside acres, even the houseboys would abandon her.

With this certain knowledge, Allison Wingfield endured the morning hour and all the interminable hours that followed it. But the solid-frame Bulldog, Clive's special Christmas gift, *did* comfort her. If the bandits killed her husband, if they stormed the bungalow in force, the gun was her one and only protection, her escape.

At night she would lie under the gauze watching the insects congregate in the corner of the ceiling, wondering if she would have the will power to pull that trigger, mulling over the method, debating where she would place the muzzle of the revolver – if she could do it at all.

Details of outrages were common knowledge. The daughter of Pat and Roy Laye had been seized during a raid on a little coffee and pineapple plantation at Mullah Kwang. She had been stripped and dowsed with kerosene and set alight. She had run screaming through the ranks of estate workers, who had watched as inscrutably as they might have watched a chicken chased by a cat, while the young girl burned to death in agony before them. Pat Laye had watched the incident from inside a besieged summerhouse. Roy had been forced to pin her to the floor with his rifle to prevent her rushing out. Pat had never been the same again. Within weeks, she had been taken back to England while Roy, a shell of a man, had remained, consumed with loathing for the country and by hatred for the peasants who had watched his daughter die. When the ripening crop had been fired one night the previous month, Roy had gone out into the bush with a Sten gun and a box of dynamite and had never returned.

The atrocity had preyed on everybody's mind. The *Straits Times* had not printed all the salient facts.

Sweating profusely as the heat increased in the concrete tower, Allison watched her husband hurry from the front of the house to the waiting Land Rover. He carried one of the Vaughans under his arm and the Colt was stuck in his belt. The driver of the Land Rover was a Eurasian, Winn they called him, who commanded a high day-wage for his expertise at the wheel and for his ability to handle firearms.

Though the distance to the live rubber was no more than a half-mile, the workers were no longer expected to walk to the trees. They bundled into the open truck, a big, burly Bedford with an unhealthy engine, and braced themselves for the ride. The Bedford was driven by a Malay who had come up, again at a high wage, from KL where he had worked as a driver for the Chinese adviser until the position had been vacated.

Allison leaned on the parapet.

For ambush attacks this was not the moment of maximum danger. The CTs would wait until the tappers were at work out in the sections, but if the bandits were here in strength and planned an assault on the compound, they would come as soon as Clive, the Land Rover and the truck were out of sight. It did not seem to deter the terrorists to realise that the defences were strong and that the Lewis gun, in its elevated position, gave excellent covering fire. Clive had told her that the terrorists considered themselves brave, in spite of the bald fact that they slaughtered women and children and unarmed men and struck without warning under cover of night.

Led by the armoured Land Rover, the Bedford nosed away from the compound towards the gate in the inner wire fence, which had been unpadlocked and stood open.

Allison backed away from the parapet and tugged the green canvas cover from the Lewis gun. Straining, she lifted the awkward ugly weapon as if it was a goat, all legs, and placed it on the upper platform of teak-wood, braced against chocks. She manhandled two sandbags into place behind the gun and stood by the assembly. She had a field of fire which extended through 180°

and covered all of the compound, the head of the Port Kernan road, the workers' lines and the sandbagged and trenched garden below the steps of the bungalow.

Tense now, her body dappled with perspiration, the woman waited for the first singing whine of bullets from the bush. The fact that she had seen nothing meant nothing. CTs were invariably invisible, using cover with a skill amounting to brilliance, aided by camouflaged combat rigs, dyed or distempered to blend with the rubber.

The Land Rover pulled out of the gate. The Bedford lurched on the rutted ground and came through. The Tamil Indian whose job it was to lock the gate of the compound strode forward. She could see Clive leaning from the passenger window of the Land Rover, elbow, shoulder, his head turned round. He would not go on until the gate was secured and the domestics – in theory – safe behind the wire.

If it was going to come it would come now.

Allison's lips compressed with the strain of waiting, waiting for the muffled crack of the rifle or the *woof* of a flare which would signal ambush. 'Ambush alley' Clive called that narrow neck of jeep track, the path from the compound, past the high stakes of the bungalow fence, into the standing trees.

The Tamil was at the gate, fumbling with padlock and key.

Children by the water taps watched the departure, new every morning. They did not wave.

No rifle shot, no flare.

Allison Wingfield licked her dry lips.

There was a two-second pause between the rattle of the shell's expulsion and its explosion.

Allison was confused. She had never heard a mortar before.

She was watching the gate, not the compound. She did not see the shape of the shell's arc in the air, but the sudden spray of dirt, and screaming, snapped her attention to the spot. The missile ploughed into a low earth wall left of the far-away water tap and showered the queue of children with dust and shrapnel.

Breath choked in the woman's lungs. Her loins constricted. Second and third shells were discharged; exploded by the taps.

The manic stutter of submachine-guns was loud along the tree-line west of the inner fence. The Land Rover heaved, plunged forward, veered. The Bedford's open deck was transformed into chaos as the tappers swarmed out of it to take cover.

Sagging backwards, Allison sat down on the sandbags. She groped for the machine-gun's spade grip. Automatically she cocked her forefinger through the chain which held the safety lock and yanked it out. Clive hadn't purchased the gun through orthodox channels and it had taken him three months to trace the type of weapon he wanted. It was fed by a two-tier pan magazine which was easy to change and was rock-solid on a tripod which gave a depression of 80° and an elevation of 85°. From the tower Allison could cover any object which lay more than thirty yards from the bungalow steps.

The woman began firing.

She had fired the gun in heat a dozen times before. Its easy action did not unsettle her. Immediately she felt better, more controlled, as she strafed the area from which the mortar shells had come. She could not, of course, direct fire anywhere near the compound or to her immediate left, where the tappers were dropping off the Bedford and heading – not for the lines, oddly – into the stand of young rubber.

There seemed to be nothing special about the attack. It had all the hallmarks of the usual sort of ambush, apart from the addition of the mortar. She realised now that it *was* a mortar. She was angered by the sophistication of the terrorists. She settled on the sandbag, handgrip drawn in against her stomach, and pumped out short bursts of 7.7mm cartridges, scanning the trees for identifiable targets.

Behind and below she heard Tavvi on the stairs. He had sense enough to call out to her so that she would not be panicked into shooting him with the Bulldog. His dark lugubrious face appeared above the trap and he shoved six ammo pans across the wooden floor towards the firing platform.

He cried, 'Many, many come this time, Miss!'

'Where are they?'

'Back place. Many, many!'

'How many?'

'Twenty times so many.'

'Go back, Tavvi. Go down and see that the kitchen is held.'

It was the house they were after. The mortar shells had been a diversion. This morning the bungalow was the target. White *tuans* and their families were always the big prize.

Allison wondered if she could somehow get the gun across the little floor and find a prop-spot for it on the other side. The slant of the tile roof would limit its tilt-angle. She doubted if she could get any sort of decent range of fire at all.

At the back of the house was a long stretch of garden, dug but not lately planted. It was hemmed by the best stretch of wire on the whole estate, not barbed wire but chain-link, ten feet high. She hoped that the houseboys wouldn't buckle under the threat. If they held their positions, the stances that Clive had picked for them, it would take a very large force of CTs indeed to storm the fence successfully. But the presence of mortars was worrying. Never before had the CTs used anything but anti-personnel weapons and occasional grenades.

The dreadful suspicion that this was no 'keep-them-on-their-toes' raid began to creep up on Allison. Finger on the trigger of the Lewis gun she leaned over the parapet to her right side and glanced back along the unfenced area towards the trees. The sun was bladed behind the leaves, cleft by the hump of the jungle-clad hill. She shaded her eyes and glimpsed darting shapes, three, four, five or them. Involuntarily she slapped the red leather holster by her side then turned again to face the compound.

The driver of the truck had reversed it, like a damned blithering fool. He had lost control and rammed it into the side of the gate. The fencing sagged inward like a folded sail. The Land Rover, with Clive's arm jutting from the open window, was swerving around the inner fence and heading down the avenue of beaten earth between the thin rubber and the head of the Port Kernan road.

It looked, at first, wonderfully controlled and heroic; the *tuan* putting himself between the enemy and his people, drawing the heavy fire. But the Land Rover straightened out and accelerated.

Its weight – all that steel plate – seemed to pile up behind the thrashing engine. Allison could hear nothing except the clash of its engine and gearbox. She saw that Clive intended to crash the breast-high check-gate at the connection of the compound fences and head on to the Port Kernan road.

She leapt to her feet, raising one arm, shouting, 'Clive, come back! Come back!'

It did not occur to Allison Wingfield that her husband might have calculated the odds and was doing the only thing possible under the circumstances – making a bold run for assistance. Telephone wires would be cut, of course, and radio communications with the police HQ at Port Kernan were erratic at best. If Clive had had more time to consider it might have dawned on him that the bandits would surely have blocked the road to the town. But only a couple of minutes had elapsed since the first mortar shell had exploded and Clive, on ground level, had been obliged to make instant decisions.

The woman watched the Land Rover breach the gate. Its fender tore through the wire and scattered the wooden frames as if they were matchwood. The Land Rover was now three or four hundred yards from the bungalow and bulling on down an apparently empty road.

From the kitchen quarters below came the sharp snap of rifle bullets. In numbed derangement, still under the illusion that Clive had fled, Allison stood on the sandbags to watch the Land Rover disappear.

The last she saw of her husband was his thin pale arm wagging and waving from the offside window.

The mine – one of a series of six – went off, triggering others. The roadway vanished in a curtain of dirt which climbed up to the height of the trees and hung there, umber and beige, stippled with red rocks which fell stunningly as the drape folded and thinned and billowed back along the road surface into the compound.

The woman pressed her breasts against the top of the parapet and shouted her husband's name.

Shots nicked the concrete right and left of her but she was

oblivious to them, gaping at the pall of dirt and smoke as it dispersed.

The Land Rover had been flung on its side. Steel plates had been ripped from its flanks and the front wheel, sheared by direct blast, hobbled and bounced down the roadway, lagging and spinning and falling even as she watched it. The CTs were fully aware of who rode in the armoured vehicle. They had sought to destroy it seven times before. Now they had it, and they had no intention of allowing Wingfield to escape alive.

Allison fell behind the Lewis gun. She hunched her shoulders and tipped the barrel. Sighting as Clive had taught her to do, she opened fire again.

A horde of little men with faces like clenched fists boiled out of the trees. They sprayed the Land Rover with submachine-gun bullets but did not converge on it. She saw the glint of the morning sun on the glass of petrol bombs as they were lobbed into the wreckage, then the bandits were running again, falling into single file along the broken wire, firing at the women and children who, mute as stumps, more or less stood where they were waiting to be mown down.

In a snarl of yellow flame, embroidered by purple smoke, the Land Rover hopped and stirred like a gigantic piece of popcorn on a grid as the glass bombs burst within. Fire roared and scythed outwards, glowed like molten gold about the blackening ribs of the machine. There was no hope for Clive now.

Allison sucked in breath. The taint of seared metal and burned flesh came with it.

Calculatingly she opened fire again.

If the workers' families were too stupid to move . . . She traversed the muzzle of the Lewis gun on a track from the shacks' end and with intense satisfaction saw several of the little yellow swine cavort, twist and fall. She saw them writhe on the scattered dirt, very clear and distinct against the raging bulk of the Land Rover. She fired again, fired until the pan ran out. She changed the pan cleanly and efficiently and fired, trailing the edge of the rubber then swinging the gun without releasing the trigger, across the road and up the rubber on the north side.

The hammering of the machine-gun deafened her. Its powerful, vital strength in her hands shook both fear and sorrow out of her mind. She had a job to do, the job that Clive had given her. She would defend the bungalow, heart of the Wade-Wingfield, would defend it until all the tappers and their families had been slaughtered and the shacks fired and the trucks burned and the trees themselves put to the torch. She would keep the Communists out of her home while there was a breath in her body. It was the least she could to to honour the memory of the man she had married in all good faith and whose manner of dying she abhorred.

Allison didn't hear the fight in the kitchen garden or the cessation of rifle fire beneath her perch. In a cold blind rage she was encapsulated in blood lust which made her shout with glee at every certain hit. Unheeding she swept the Lewis gun this way and that, saw the swine retreat and congregate, the dead and dying writhing on the ground.

Allison didn't hear the trap open.

The first she knew of the taking of the tower was when an arm went round her throat and another round her waist and she was pulled backwards from the bags.

She groped for the butt of the Bulldog in its leather holster but the soldier was too quick for her. He put his knee on her shoulder and held her spreadeagled before him.

Through streaky sweat and tears, Allison stared into the upside-down features.

'Captain Deacon?' she gasped, in disbelief.

'At your service, Mrs Wingfield.'

4 Ring of fire

Big Buz Campbell crouched by a pile of cut timber fifty yards from the smokehouse on the north side of the compound. He paused there long enough to whip off his beret and swab his face and hands with it. He didn't want greasy fingers to spoil his aim. Every goddamned shot would have to count now, the odds being as they were. Another twenty minutes on arrival time would have made all the difference. But they had got there only ten minutes or so before the balloon went up and had had no opportunity to find the best rifle sites. Anyhow the bloody CTs were out in force. The little sonsabitches were everywhere. Front, back and flanks. This was no fast in-and-out attack. This Wei Sand Shan gink sure meant business, meant to lay waste to the plantation every which way.

'How many do you figure, wee man?'

'Couple o' hundred,' said P.B.

'Right.'

The gun on the roof sounded heavy. From what he could see from the rear, it was doing a helluva lot of damage to the bandits who had staged the frontal assault. But the house was vulnerable to the bunch who had infiltrated the open store huts on the edge of the paddi. Twenty of them, and they'd sure have had the bungalow by now if Deke and his merry men hadn't happened along. The guy who owned this piece of real estate could thank his lucky stars that Deacon had guessed right.

The CTs were staging something big and noisy at the front of the place. Campbell's guess was that it was only a diversion to enable the smaller unit to storm the kitchen and peg the bungalow. Kitchen gardens had been stomped flat to provide an open area between the outbuildings and the house itself. Whoever had set up the defences had been pretty smart. High chain-link fences would make it difficult for the raiders to slink into the garden. There was rifle fire, though not enough of it, from the windows of the house itself; a home guard, kind of, probably made up of the domestic staff.

But the mortar had been a surprise.

The operation was smooth and well rehearsed. Deacon claimed that Sand Shan was cutting his military teeth on this operation. Swamping the Wade-Wingfield was an object lesson to other planters in the district. Banner headline stuff: burned-out hulks and mutilated corpses. No penny-ante game now, whatever it had been before.

The CTs were too spread to allow snipers to pick them off. Within a minute of the battle start, that much became obvious.

Deacon had been quick to alter his plan.

'I'm going for the house,' he said. 'There may be a radio. We need help – and fast. Johnny, take the Dyak and find a spot on the left side of the building. Keep as near as you can to the bungalow. That's our fall-back point. There's just too many out there for us to sift into the jungle.'

'You want P.B. and me to take the right?' said Buz.

'Absolutely.'

'Who's in the house?'

'Wingfield's wife.'

'Where's Wingfield?'

'Although we can't see him, I suspect he just started his morning round. That's probably what the racket was.'

'What if there is not a radio?' Badhur had asked.

'Then we'll just have to pray the bandits think there's more of us than there is – and pull out.'

'Hold as long as we can,' said Buz, 'then withdraw to the bungalow?'

'Exactly.'

'Deacon's last stand, eh?' said P.B.

'I sincerely hope not,' Deacon retorted.

Deacon's run for the bungalow was rendered hairy by the sudden advance of bandits on the garden fence. No fool, the SAS captain picked his route carefully, keeping out of the fire lines from the windows above the step-like verandah. Glass in the windows of the bungalow had been shattered but wooden shutters were roped down at angles and the place had the look of a fortress about it. The front of the verandah, both sides of a flight of shallow, wooden steps, had been packed with sand; not bags, which rotted quickly in this climate, but a sand-gravel-clay mix which made a good ground-level barricade and would stop anybody slithering under the building.

It wasn't until P.B. and he made the wood pile that Buz noticed the fire slots in the wall. Timber-shored, too. He could even see the glint of sunlight on the rifle barrels which poked through. Inside would be a root cellar which Wingfield had turned into a shooting gallery. Pretty smart, Buz thought again.

The bandits had sent eight men to take the fence. The chain-link had been holed by three or four shells from the mortar in the rubber to the far right; a two-inch trench mortar by the grunt of it, capable of slinging a two-pounder some four hundred yards at a rate of five shells per minute. But the Commies weren't chucking them in near that fast, seemed to be eking them out. Maybe they were short of ammo. After all, they had trekked the stuff in and would have had to back-pack the artillery too.

As he watched the first wave of CTs scuttle from the cover of the barn-like hut and head towards the fence, Buz wondered if it was like this throughout Malaya, if all the goddamned planters lived like prisoners. He had been in the country less than a month and had seen more atrocities than he had done in a year in Normandy and Scandinavia, even in the desert.

Commies weren't after your land or your bread; they were after your life. Must be like living in Indian territory in the days of the Old West, never knowing when the Apaches were going to go on the warpath and come down in search of scalps. If the Dyak, P.B.'s buddy, was anything to go by, the natives here didn't stop at scalps; they took your head and all.

P.B. hissed, 'What're we waitin' for, Buz?'

'We've gotta give the Deke a chance to reach the side of the house.'

'They haven't spotted him yet.'

'Yeah, I know.'

'Soon's them bastards reach the wire . . .'

'Sure,' said Buz, soothingly. 'They're all yours, wee man.'

The Deke, far left, was about sixty yards off, forty from the gable of the bungalow. Jesus, if a bunch of CTs appeared around the corner from the front yard now Deacon would be up shit creek.

P.B. said, 'Here they come.'

They were fast as fleas, hopping out of the rubber trees, young stuff by the size of it. You could hardly make out the Chinks, like God had painted their complexions as camouflage. They weren't yellow. Close to being tallow-coloured. None older than twenty-five, they all looked alike at the distance.

So far, SAS detail 'Gable' hadn't fired a shot.

They still had the element of surprise on their side, even if they had fucked up a bit by coming in too cautiously from the outland. Sand Shan hadn't left patrols out there; he had converged every bandit at his command in the vicinity of the bungalow and the compound; what was called a concentrated attack. Target warfare.

Screaming mingled with the firing of a lot of guns. Buz glanced at P.B. who was, or seemed, oblivious. The Scot, for the first time in nearly six years, was sinking into the trance which preceded a killing action. Buz had been privileged to see it many times before. P. B. McNair was the best goddamned rifle shot in the whole British Army, or had been half a dozen years back. Natural aptitude plus a lot of practice kept the wee man sharp, but it was his ability to become one with the rifle which made him so lethal. So goddamned relaxed, even his eyelids looked heavy while he did the little chores that every good sniper performed before opening up shop.

'How many you think you can take?'

'Hmmm?' P.B. crooned. 'As many's I can see.'

Buz said, 'Deke's got nothin' but clearway. He's waitin' for you.'

'Aye, right,' said P.B. 'Bugger off, Buz, eh.'

Buz was not insulted. He grinned and slunk backwards out of the shadow of the pile of loose timber. P.B. was on the button. Two men in the position was one too many.

Buz crept backwards. The pale grass which sprouted around that part of the yard gave excellent cover, provided he kept his ass down. He had a fine angle on the set-up now. Deacon was in position by a water cistern, ready to cut across the diagonal to the point where the chain-link fence met the gable of the bungalow. P.B. was snuggled by the woodpile, ready to do his number not with the Mauser but with Lee Enfield rifle No. 5, Mark 1 which, appropriately, was nicknamed the 'jungle carbine' because the weapon came fitted with a knife-type bayonet, an unusual feature on sniping rifles. Badhur and the Dyak had disappeared into the jungle skirt, heading for the rubber by the south-east side of the compound. From the bungalow came occasional shots which didn't sound convincing.

Buz raised his head and made a quick recce. Flashes from the house; no return fire yet. Like the Deke the CTs were fixing to get themselves into a sprint position before they opened up.

The pace of the attack was accelerating. The racket from round front of the bungalow was puzzling and when a big bang split the humidity Buz ducked his head immediately.

Jesus! Had they hauled in field-pieces?

Memories rose to the surface of his brain like debris from a muddy lake. Yeah, something had run smack into a minefield. Up on the roof of the house the Lewis gun went nutty, yammering out an endless stream of bullets. And at that same moment the forward-position Commies stormed the chain-link.

A line of a dozen or so of their brethren advanced with caution from the store barns, giving covering fire. Buz knew what he had to do. Oh, yeah. What a peachy idea. What a great goddamned opportunity!

Ignoring the action which had flared in the garden and surrounding yards, the sergeant slid backwards once more and turning his rump to the fighting headed at a crouched run for the fringe of the old paddi, close to the spot where the SAS unit had emerged from the jungle a half-hour ago. Since most of the bandits were at the front of the bungalow, and the twenty-man detail set to sneak the house from the back were on the move, Buz doubted if he would bump into Reds in the jungle edge. As soon as he hit the tall cover he got to his feet and ran like hell, veering hard left.

The ground rose slightly, enough to give him a view of the compound.

Smoke soaring over the roof of the house told him that the CTs had fired the workers' lines. The arc-lamps had gone out. One of them was twisted at a weird angle, victim of a mortar shell. Buz took in all this visual data peripherally. What he was trying to deduce was where the Commies had gotten to in relation to the chain-link. Then he had it, a clear view. Panting, he stopped, slumped against a tree and look across the clearway.

P.B. had sure done his number. Commies were hanging dead against the blown wire like skunk-skins. Kneeling and prone, the back-up men had switched their fire-power to the woodpile. Buz reckoned, however, that P.B. was long gone from there, and that Deke had made it to the house.

Buz didn't tarry. He plunged on towards the store huts, open-sided barns where timber for the smokehouse ovens was stashed.

Sun was up now, the haze going out of the atmosphere. The smell of burning reached him, distinct and acrid. The Lewis gun was beating away at a helluva lick. The Commies' answering fire sounded louder. His own field of fire, an open stretch of scrub and earth-pad between the wing of the huts and the fence, was bathed in sunlight. The CTs, about a dozen of them, were in single stations and in pairs, grabbing up what cover they could. Buz had no notion of where P.B. had slithered to, but the Commies seemed to have some sort of target in view and were hammering away with subs and carbines. Maybe at the woodpile, maybe not.

Buz did not doubt that P.B. was free and clear and on the loose.

Buz got himself into a clump of stinking green weeds by the side of the store huts' eastern uprights. He looked up at the buckled slats of the roof. Not thatch. Weathered boards. A cluster of small birds, like swallows, twittered about the rafters. Old ropes, like vines, dangled from the beams. There didn't appear to be much under the roof: a rusted tractor and a couple of aluminium feed-bins around which the swallows had been pecking when he disturbed them. From the stinking clump a lizard a foot long shot away from the sergeant's boots, startling him. He got down into the clump and spread the weapons by his side.

Six grenades.

Sten. Three magazines.

Dagger, bayonet-type.

Enough.

The firing from the house had all but ceased. Christ knew what was happening round front. It was like playing the scene behind the backcloth of a theatre stage. But the bandits still hadn't made him and lay wide open before him.

Buz didn't rush things. He waited, grenade in each hand, until he picked up P.B.'s position. P.B. had retreated to the cistern which Deacon had used as a way-stage on his run for the house. Buz couldn't see P. B. McNair, of course, not even the flash of the Lee Enfield. But he could tell where his compadre had holed out by the reactions of the bandits, and the manner in which they died.

It was less easy for a sniper, even one as hot as P.B., when he was pinned down by retaliatory fire and didn't have a strong position. Even so, three, then four of the bandits went down. They knew they were under attack themselves but must have figured it to be local talent on the end of the rifle, not an army mob. Otherwise surely they'd have checked their backs.

Buz grinned.

Sitting-duck time in Dixie?

Oh, yeah!

With a rifle he could have notched up the whole bag. But he didn't have a rifle. The hot sun sizzled. The weeds stank like hot horse-piss. Sweat beaded the sergeant's brow. He mopped it off with the beret, watching alertly all the while.

The bandits were trying to regroup, to push down the back aisle to the northern corner of the chain-link. P.B. wouldn't have an angle on them. Buz congratulated himself on his bright idea and chuckled as another of the solo guns tumbled and lay crucified on the ground. How many left? Only six. No sign of reinforcements coming round the house yet. Maybe the Lewis gun had tied them up. Maybe the leader, Shan, reckoned he just had to hang about and let his laddies do the job.

Four terrorists had gotten themselves into a huddle off to the right. Any guy with half a brain could have figured out their intentions.

Buz stole forward. There were two grenade targets within reasonable range. The distance to the house was only three hundred yards. He could reach the mortar team with the grenades. Sure enough, the crew was setting up the weapons, its barrel aimed at P.B.'s hide. Wasting no time now, Buz hung the Sten around his neck and packed the magazines into the pouch along with the spare grenades.

Bands of shadow marked the floor of the barn, zebra-striped. Buz crabbed through them, making a narrow angle narrower. He would be visible now if any of the Commies looked in his direction. Firing from the rear of the bungalow had ceased. Even the Lewis gun was silent. Sounded like a wind-down all round.

The mortar crew, with a shell in the tube, were dickering with the range. He couldn't wait a moment longer.

The sergeant came out running. He made twenty yards then hurled the grenade with a high, slinging, overarm action. He didn't hit the deck. He lobbed a second grenade from his left hand into his right, took another five steps and pitched it after the first. Then he went down, due right, rolling, as the missiles sailed through sunlight and landed. P.B. couldn't have failed to see what he'd done. The wee man would be on the shuffle, seizing the opportunity to better his position.

Buz hit the dirt.

The grenades exploded rapidly one after the other. The mortar and its crew of four took the full blast. It had been a mighty long throw. Buz was pleased to have struck target. He screwed himself round and lying at full length kicked the dirt into a little mound with his boots and scrambled back to it, immediately had the Sten propped and firing.

P.B. had gone off like a hare, zigzagging.

The remaining bandits were exposed in a crossfire which wiped them out within twenty seconds.

Buz got up and ran down the side of the yard towards the north corner of the chain-link fence. P.B. was over by the other end, south-west. In the open area back of the kitchen garden, the bandits lay dead or dying. There was no last gasp from any of them, though a couple tried to drag themselves off, mewing like crushed kittens.

Buz could see the bungalow windows, enigmatic slots of shadow, gelid under hinged shutters. He hoped to Christ some trigger-happy houseboy wasn't lining up on him in the mistaken impression that he was a Chink. Nothing appeared to be moving in there. He signalled to P.B. who, by the far corner of the building, was peering up at the roof.

The guy came inching down the roof on his tailbone, a tall dark-skinned Tamil with a horse-face drawn by fear. He carried no weapons and Buz didn't figure him for a Commie.

Buz yelled, 'What's happenin' in there?'

The Tamil rolled his eyes at the sergeant and kept on coming, dragging his ass down the slanted tiles. He wasn't that high off the ground, twenty-five feet maybe. Above the Indian there was a helluva lot of smoke in the sky. It came home to Buz right there and then that Sand Shan was in possession of the main compound and any second now would have a bunch of his bandits round back.

Buz yelled again, 'What the fuck's happenin'?'

The Tamil had reached the edge of the roof. The newly painted iron guttering gave him a toe-hold. He squatted, hands on knees, eyes glued to the wooden verandah which was hardly wider than a step-top.

Buz was still outside the chain-link. He could sense the jungle and the rubber trees at his back. He was as exposed here as a prisoner in an execution yard. Frig the goddamned gutless Indian! He had to get inside the house or into jungle cover pretty goddamned quick.

'Jump, man. Jump,' P.B. shouted to the Tamil.

The Scot was hanging on to the chain-link on the far side of the compound. He was more exposed there than Buz, what with the curve of the track to the southern sectors lying behind him.

The Tamil remained frozen in abject terror.

What happened next caught Buz by surprise. Suddenly the screen-door of the bungalow's kitchen burst open. Buz dived as a couple of Indians, younger than the guy on the roof, bolted out.

They weren't escaping: one carried a rifle, an old bolt-action piece; the other had a beautiful Vaughan shotgun wagging about in his right hand.

Buz shouted, 'Hold it right there!'

But the Indians were mad and spooked, and obviously knew he was British and wouldn't cut them down in cold blood. They dove off the verandah steps, the door clattering behind them, swung round and chattered at the guy on the roof. He shook his head; shook his head until his eyes seemed to rattle like dice. The houseboys jabbered and chattered, then, with no indication what was on their minds, riddled the roof-squatter with bullets and shot.

The act was shocking and inexplicable.

Almost sawn in half by the shotgun, duck pants and cream linen jacket splashed with blood, the Tamil toppled. He dropped with a soggy thud to the ground. If he hadn't been dead when he left the roof, he was dead for sure a split second after he struck. Buz could hear the snap of his neck bone loud as a pistol shot.

P.B. sprinted the length of the wire, the Enfield trained on the crazy Indians who now that part of it was done had started chattering at each other.

P.B. came abreast of Buz.

'Bloody bleedin' hell, what was yon all about?'

'Christ knows!'

'They Commies, d'you think?'

The younger of the Indian servants – not exactly a boy, Buz noticed – spun on his heel and strode to the fence. He was lucky not to get a bullet in his head doing that. He wagged the shotgun again; a really beautiful weapon, identical to one Buz had once owned before it was pinched during a para drop on Bruges.

The houseboy bowed and, still gibbering, said, 'Tavvi was bad man. He work for bandit leader, you do understand?'

'What's he sayin'?' asked P.B.

'Bad, bad man. He sell us to Shan, do you see?'

'Yeah, yeah!' said Buz.

'Scupper radio. Now we stuck. Cannot call policemen from town to come save us.'

'Listen, Jim,' said P.B. 'Open the bloody gate, eh?'

'Yes, I will do so. Yes, yes.'

In spite of its padlock, the upright gate in the chain-link fence had not been locked at all. The Indian with the rifle had it open in no time.

The Indian houseboys were scared shitless but they weren't mad now. They had contributed to the morning's battle and had taken their own peculiar revenge. It wasn't until later Buz learned that the Tamil on the roof had indeed sold the occupants of the bungalow up river. He hadn't counted on the SAS popping out of the jungle. He had been Wei Sand Shan's 'inside' connection. Still he hadn't quite delivered all he was supposed to, for the Lewis gun was supposed to have been sabotaged too. But the guy *had* got to the radio, and he *had* left the back gate open – and had probably supplied Sand Shan with all the gen required to time the big raid.

He didn't look like much, that tall, skinny Indian, lying there on the ground by the high step, his head twisted and blood seeping out of his body into the thirsty earth. But he had done the dirt on his buddies, which was unusual for a Tamil Indian, and they hated him for collaborating with Chinese. It sure was something for a Tamil to kill a brother, and the pair of assassins were beginning to realise just what they'd done.

Buz went through the open gate followed by P.B. The houseboys bowed again then, without even a word of goodbye, sprinted out of the garden and headed past the corpses of the Commies straight for the open huts.

'After you, Claude,' said P.B., jerking his Enfield towards the screen-door.

'Yeah,' said Buz Campbell as he stepped cautiously into the kitchen of the Wingfields' bungalow.

Johnny Badhur reached the shelter of the rubber on the corner of the south and east sections of the Wade-Wingfield. At last he had a clear view of the compound. He was aggrieved and dismayed by what he saw. Any doubts which he still harboured regarding Wei Sand Shan's commitment to wipe out the plantation vanished.

The workers' lines had been put to the torch. The truck had been set alight and something – a jeep, perhaps – had been blown up on the Port Kernan road.

Johnny had seen the results of terrorist action before but only in isolation: one car, a couple of shacks, two or three corpses, the small and ineffectual gestures of a regime which, Johnny believed, would peter out as soon as it was seriously opposed.

There had been, to his sure knowledge, no full-scale organised assault like the one on the Wade-Wingfield. It was apparent that Wei Sand Shan would be satisfied with nothing less than a 'victory', which in the terminology of the times meant slaughter. Already the compound was scattered with wounded. The crying of children was pitiful, a haunting low-key chant below the roar of kerosene torches and the crackle of flames in the blocks.

Squatting on his haunches, the Dyak by his side, Johnny surveyed the results of the CTs' raid. The value of surprise coupled with force was being thoroughly proved. He wondered which of the knots of men in combat rig contained Sand Shan, if it would be possible to identify and kill the leader of the horror-mongers.

Johnny Badhur was not above martyrdom.

As if reading his thoughts, the Dyak glowered into his face and shook his head scowling. In the earth between his feet the Dyak drew a picture with the point of his knife; a map of sorts. Johnny peered at it as the knife-tip completed the design.

He asked, 'What do you mean, Umgah?'

In Malayan the Dyak said, 'We run. You, me.'

'Run? Good God! Are you not warrior? I am warrior. Not run.'

Impatiently, the knife jabbed the dirt again.

'Many warriors. Go. See. We go run-run quick, Gurkha. You, me. Bring soldiers here.'

Johnny saw what the Dyak meant. Tribal wars and savage deeds in the jungles of Borneo and Sarawak had inculcated in Umgah a healthy respect for weight of numbers.

There was no hope now of 'saving' the compound. The bandits were in full possession and controlled the egress road. He understood the Dyak's map; the curving line represented the road to the town. It would take at the best four hours to reach Port Kernan on foot.

Umgah drew more lines in the dirt.

Johnny nodded. A couple of miles through the rubber, which was not hard going, and they would emerge on the road below the bend, hidden from the bandits – unless the bandits had set up patrols further west, which was possible but not probable.

Johnny did not hesitate. There was no time to waste. The Dyak was correct. The best thing to do would be to have a shot at rousing SAS 'A' Squadron from barracks at the Port, though it would take hours for help to arrive and Johnny was not certain that the bungalow could be held that long. To try to sneak back to it, to join the others within its walls, however, would be stupid. It might be half a day or more before suspicions in town prompted somebody to come out to check on the Wingfields, by which time there would be nothing left.

Johnny made a signal. The Dyak and he withdrew from the edge of the rubber. Falling back into the arched trees, they headed around the compound towards the Port Kernan road.

Before it was finally blotted from view Johnny took one last look at the bungalow. Sitting high and isolated on a spur of the open ground there was something awfully English about it in spite of the great drapery of trees and the hot yellow sky. In the tower he could just make out two figures. One of them, he felt sure, would be Captain Deacon. Who better to hold the outpost against seige?

Hoisting the filthy rucksack on to his shoulders the Dyak pulled Johnny away.

The wifie, P.B. thought, looked like she'd been wrung through a mangle. Her hair was teased out, her cheeks glowed red, her face was stained with sweat, tears and dust, her clothing was soiled and rumpled. Even at that she was a bonnie, sonsy piece of crumpet. P.B. wished he'd got there first, though he wasn't her class, and it was Deacon she fancied anyhow. Anybody with half an eye could tell that the Wingfield wifie thought Captain Jeff Deacon was the bee's knees.

The bungalow was a lot bigger than it looked from outside. Long cool rooms lay along a corridor. There was food in the kitchen. Buz and P.B. helped themselves to oranges from a bowl on the way past. There was nobody downstairs. A wee trap in the polished wood floor opened to a cellar which smelled dank, like the Glasgow Underground.

Buz shouted, 'Captain Deacon! We're here!

'Upstairs, Buz!' came the answer.

Buz didn't go upstairs right away. He signalled to P.B. and the soldiers skipped through the house to the living-room. There was a bow-fronted bar in one corner, lots of books in shelves against the wall, and a big gramophone with a handle on a stand close by a wickerwork chair.

P.B. eyed the bottles behind the bar but contented himself with sucking juice from an orange while Buz nosed around and scouted the disposition of the enemy from the window.

Rectangles of thick glass, flower-patterned curtains on bamboo rods, a gigantic sofa covered in patterned chintz; Buz pressed himself against the curtains. One of the windows had been smashed. Glass sparkled on the polished floor, blown all over the bloody place. Surprisingly the other window was intact. P.B. got himself on the side of it, opposite the Sergeant. He sucked the orange dry and dropped the remains, then touched back the curtain with the snout of his rifle.

'Jesus!' P.B. muttered.

The workers' lines were burning fiercely. Heavy smoke curled across the compound, obscuring the head of the main road. There was a garden at an easy slope. Below it bandits were getting themselves into position. The Lewis gun didn't seem to be finding marks now, though the Communists' cover was poor.

'How many mortars you figure they've got?' Buz called.

'Couple, maybe more.'

'Men?'

'Hard t'say. Looks like a fuckin' battalion t'me.'

'Wonder where the Gurkha's gotten to.'

'If he saw this,' said P.B., 'an' he's wise, he'll have headed for town.'

'Long friggin' way to town,' said Buz.

P.B. shrugged. He didn't much care about the Gurkha and had forgotten all about the Dyak. He was thinking about how much ammo he had and how long he could hold the front of the bungalow. There was no firing. The bandits didn't seem to be in any particular hurry. Why should they be, twenty miles from a barracks, with the road sewn up and telephone wires down and the emergency short-wave knocked out?

'Somebody'll hear the rumpus,' said P.B.

'Doubt it, wee man. This is the jungle, remember.'

P.B. shrugged again. 'Aye, so it is.'

The Lewis gun stopped. Seconds later Deacon came into the living-room along with the woman. P.B. had a good swatch at her. Dishevelled though she was, and washed out, she was a stunner. More important than the size of her tits was the red leather gun-belt at her waist and the hard, pursed sort of look on her biscuit. She reminded P.B. of posh women who used to travel alone on sleeping-car expresses, who bossed you about something chronic but gave you the eye as if they wanted you to try it on, were daring you to do it to them.

Deacon said, 'Buz, P.B., this is Mrs Wingfield.'

Buz nodded, 'Ma'am.'

P.B. said nothing. The woman took Deacon's arm, holding him for comfort. She gave the soldiers a funny wee bow.

Deacon said, 'It's Mrs Wingfield's property, so I request you to treat it with respect.'

P.B. glanced at Buz and gave him a round eye. Respect? God, the bloody Commies would blast the shit out of the building. In five or ten minutes they'd be struggling to save their necks, never mind the furniture.

Deacon said, 'I assume you realise what's happening?'

'Sure,' said the Sergeant. 'Siege in progress.'

'Sand Shan knows we're in here. He may not have learned that we're so few in number. But he'll have sent scouts into the rubber to check. He's in no real rush at the moment. He isn't so plentifully supplied with guerrillas that he can afford to swamp us. Did you eliminate the lot at the back of the house?'

'Yep,' said Buz.

'How many?'

'Twenty, thereabouts.'

'Good work,' said Deacon.

The Captain did not seem to object to the woman hanging on to his arm. P.B. sucked another orange and wiped juice from the stubble on his chin with his sleeve.

Deacon said, 'Sand Shan will select six or eight small teams. He'll probably chuck in a mortar shell or two to keep us low, then send in the teams three or four at a time.'

'Can we cover them all?' the woman asked.

She sounded calm, with a low, sexy voice.

Deacon said, 'In fact, Allison, no.'

'I can handle a rifle.'

'I'm sure you can,' said Deacon. 'You certainly handled the Lewis very competently.'

Buz said, 'Better stow the gab, Deke.'

'Absolutely,' Deacon agreed. 'P.B., stay put. Cover the front and left flank. Buz, take the rear of the house. Allison, will you put yourself in the south-facing room which has, if I recall, only a small window.'

'Where will you be?'

'On the roof.'

'How much ammo you got for that gun?' Buz asked.

'Not nearly enough.'

'Ain't there more?'

'Our . . . our servant, an Indian,' said Allison, 'he . . .'

'Yeah, we know about him. Shan's man. He's chopped. The other boys got him. Served the sonuvabitch right. Seems he nobbled the radio.'

'I . . . I don't know where he's hidden the spare magazines,' said Allison.

Buz unstrapped the canvas grenade pouch from his shoulder and passed it to Deacon. 'Take these. P.B., unload your spuds.'

P.B. handed over four grenades. He wasn't much of a one for grenades anyway. He preferred the precision of the rifle or the accuracy of the bayonet.

'We can hold the square room at the bottom of the stairs,' said Deacon. 'And, if necessary, even retreat to the cellar.'

'What happened t'the Gurkha?' P.B. inquired as he pushed the sofa towards the window.

'Haven't a clue,' said Deacon. 'My one hope is that Johnny sized up the situation and set off for help.'

'How far's the nearest outpost with a radio, ma'am?'

'Sixteen miles. The Paris Hill place. Along the Port Kernan road. Only three or four miles from the army garrison.'

'A pretty long hike,' said Buz.

'If only this was a transport day . . .' said Allison Wingfield. 'If only Clive . . .'

'Don't you have a prearranged call time for the radio?'

'Not that I'm aware of, no,' the woman replied.

'What are they up to now, P.B.?' Deacon asked.

P.B. had adjusted the long chintz-covered sofa to his satisfaction. He hadn't taken the Captain's warning about not damaging the property seriously. Christ, the Commies were out there burning everything in sight! He kneeled on the sofa and peered through the undamaged window.

'Can't see much,' he said. 'Haud on, though. Looks like they're havin' a meetin'.'

Deacon was by P.B.'s side instantly, binoculars trained.

The bandits had cleared the area immediately in front of the bungalow. They had done their work, had disposed of the transport and marched the workers away out of sight, those who were still alive. Eight Chinks scuttled out of the rubber away to the right and headed towards the main group.

'There's Sand Shan,' Deacon said.

'You sure?'

'Absolutely. It's not a face I'll ever forget.'

'What's he puttin' out?' the Scot asked.

'As I suspected,' said Deacon. 'He seems to be splitting his force into small units. He must be confident that he has us completely cut off, otherwise he would plump for a quick kill.'

'What's he after?' said P.B. 'I mean, bloody hell, Jeff, he canny know you're here.'

'Of course not,' said Deacon. 'I told you, it's in the nature of Wei Sand Shan to be thorough. He isn't going to be satisfied with half a massacre, not at this stage. He wants to issue warning to other planters and estate-owners and to their work-forces: obey or be killed.'

'Clive . . .' said Mrs Wingfield, 'Clive said he would die before he would be terrorised into leaving.'

There was a moment's silence. P.B. glanced at Deacon then, speculatively, at the woman. He wondered if she was as much in control as she seemed to be. After all she'd just seen her hubby blown up.

Deacon got up. 'All right. Best attend your posts.'

Buz had already retreated into the kitchen to seek a protected vantage point and do a bit of hauling and sorting of dressers and cupboards. Whatever happened, they had to keep the bandits out of the bungalow and hope that they could hold them off until help arrived from Port Kernan.

P.B. settled at his station. Leaning his elbows on the soft back of the sofa he had a clear view of the front of the house. As soon as the woman went away he would strip down the curtains to give himself a wider frame.

The wifie put her hand on his arm.

P.B. shot a surprised look at her.

'May I get you something to drink?' she asked.

'Aye,' said P. B. McNair.

'What?'

Conscience fought with inclination.

'Water,' the Scot said, and from the doorway he heard Deacon laugh.

Johnny Badhur's feet were bleeding now. The virus, or whatever pestilential thing it was that loved the sweat-warmed skin of the human foot, had gnawed its way through the harder outer layers in rapid order and blood had begun to ooze through the spongy pores.

Oddly, the Gurkha experienced relief when the blood came, though what sort of a mess he would be in when he reached town and got to take his boots off did not bear thinking about. He had seen men crippled by the rot, by blood-poisoning and gangrene arising from neglected conditions. He wanted to tell Umgah not to travel so fast. But that would have involved him in loss of face and being a true Gurkha he would shag on until his toes dropped off before he would admit that he could not keep up with a jungle native. He loped after the Dyak, dreaming of a chemical footbath, of sweet-smelling unguents and the hypo shots he would receive from the doctor at the base hospital at Port Kernan. While he dreamed, however, he kept right on going, trotting after the headhunter through the monotonous stands of rubber.

In half an hour or so the pair covered three miles.

The Dyak pulled to the right. They were still within the boundaries of the Wade-Wingfield and there were signs on the trees of recent tappings. Umgah was cautious but 'fast cautious', not stealthy. He ran with a rolling, skipping gait, spears crossed over his chest, the obscene haversack bouncing on his naked back, dappling the dark skin with blood.

When the Dyak paused, black flies swarmed around him.

Chest heaving, Johnny Badhur limped up to the native's side. Screened by a huge banana-leaf bush the men crouched.

Umgah lifted his upper lip and showed his teeth. It was not a smile or even a grimace but a thoughtful expression, characteristic of his tribe. With the point of the short spear he delicately scratched his nose, upper lip still lifted and the yellowish eyeballs rolled away to the right.

'Tist,' the Dyak hissed.

Though they were not far from the compound, the sounds of the CT's attack had been pillowed by the twists of the road and the density of the rubber trees. There was a faint odour of smoke; and that was all.

'Tist-tist.' hissed the Dyak again and dabbed the tip of the spear to the right. 'Rod der.'

Blood pulsed like sulphuric acid in Johnny's feet. He felt as if he was planted in two little vats of the stuff. He was in too much pain to feel fear. The noise, though, intrigued him. For a second or so he almost forgot about his decaying trotters and listened intently, head cocked.

'What is it?'

'Heh! Heh!' The Dyak chuckled. '*Berok* tekkers.'

Two boys in white shirts and khaki shorts emerged on to the main road from a side track which straggled up an incline through the thinning rubber trees. They were Malays and were pushing Raleigh bicycles. A light wooden side-car was bolted to the frame of each of the Raleighs and erected within the side-cars were chicken-wire cages some three feet in height.

Umgah did not have to explain to Johnny what the boys were up to. They had been into the jungle, into a remote valley which lay north-west of Wade-Wingfield, to capture young male macaques. Powerful brutes with short stumpy tails and dull brown fur, *beroks* were much prized as coconut retrievers. When trained they could make their owners a nice little sum by shinning up palms and picking nuts indicated by the animal's owner. *Beroks* were not common in this state. Obviously the boys had risked an encounter with CTs to obtain them.

Laughing happily and without caution the boys were making almost as much noise as the macaques. The monkeys were frightened, shook their frail cages, chattered and grunted.

Umgah laughed again. For the life of him Johnny Badhur could not see what was so amusing about two Malays and their captive *beroks*. The pain and the strain of the past days had dulled his wits. It wasn't the boys or the monkeys that tickled the Dyak.

It was the Raleigh bicycles.

'Beks. Beks. Eh? Yew. Me. Beks.'

Johnny Badhur put his hand to his brow. Of course. Rotting feet or not, he could ride a bicycle with the best of them. He gathered from Umgah's gestures that the Dyak too had acquired that skill, probably at one or other of the army barracks to which he had been attached during the war years.

'*Ting-ting*. Bek Port Ke'n. Okey?'

'Okay,' said Johnny Badhur. 'Yes, okay.'

Because they were in too much of a hurry to bargain, argue and explain, they took the bicycles at gun-point.

The Malays were startled to say the least of it, frightened of the Dyak and his bloody haversack, knowing perhaps what it contained. They relinquished the bicycles without protest and seemed more concerned that they would be permitted to keep the *beroks*.

Bedrolls and camping groundsheets were strapped to the back of the Raleighs. Johnny told the Dyak to strip them off. One of the boys had a spanner and with it he unbolted the wooden side-cars. Johnny slung the Sten on to his back and tentatively hoisted himself on to the saddle.

The coconut monkeys had fallen silent, glaring at the strangers, their brown-furred faces quizzical within the wire cages.

Johnny placed his feet on the pedals. The pressure of the metal hurt, but not badly.

The Dyak was already in motion, whirring round and round on the road, thoroughly at home on the machine, enjoying himself.

Johnny said, 'Keep out of sight, chaps. Communists have attacked the rubber plantation.'

'*Tuan* Wingfield's?'

'Yes,' said Johnny Badhur. 'That's why we need the wheels, do you see? To ride quickly for assistance.'

The boys brightened. 'Take them. Bandits bad.'

'You can pick the bicycles up at the barracks in Port Kernan,' said Johnny.

'Get the, soldier, please,' said one of the boys, shaking his fist. 'Shh . . . shh . . . shoot all the Chinese bastids.'

Johnny raised one hand in farewell, wobbled, clapped his hand back on to the rubber grip and steered out on to the hard-packed dirt on the road's shoulder, the line which Umgah had taken.

The Dyak was already two hundred yards away, back crested, buttocks in the air, riding like a star of the velodrome.

Not to be outdone by a primitive headhunter, Johnny Badhur pumped his legs. He felt the tyres bite and the wind begin to whip about him and, with the two young Malays cheering him on, he headed after the Dyak along the road to the barracks.

She would not leave him. He understood it. The Land Rover had almost burned itself out. But the charred hulk was like a monument, a visible reminder that everything had changed for her. She was a widow now, and her home, Malaya, was a hostile place. If they survived the next four or five hours, made it through to the afternoon, if Johnny and Umgah had not been picked up by Shan's bandits, then the trouble would only be beginning for Allison Wingfield.

Deacon was the connection between the fragile existence of today and the miseries of tomorrow, all the uncertainties that the future held.

He put his arm about her.

'Are you all right?'

'Perfectly fine, thank you.'

Still hugging her, the captain glanced up from the tower to the ridge of the red tile roof. It was a distance of no more than ten feet. He peeped down at the compound once more. The CTs had got under cover, more or less. Shan would be aware that they were short of ammo. The guerrilla leader's experience of packing shells through the deep jungle would tell him so. Shan would know by this time that he had been caught by a back-door play, but he would also know the limitations of it.

The woman said, 'Give me the rifle, please.'

Deacon put the rifle down on the sandbag, together with eight filled clips and a handful of cartridges in a cardboard box. He had cleaned out Clive Wingfield's armoury and had been disappointed to discover only a limited supply of ammunition, all of it in calibres unsuited to SAS weapons. Buz had claimed the Vaughan shotgun. The sergeant, Deacon remembered, had had a Vaughan of his own once. The shotgun was a marvellous weapon for short-range work.

'I wouldn't mind a scout from the rooftop,' said Deacon.

'It's too dangerous. You'd be very exposed.'

'I know. Pity.'

'In any case,' said Allison Wingfield, 'it's too late. Here they come.'

No *banzai* attack this. Crouched by a slot in the concrete wall, Deacon watched the guerrillas advance along the avenue by the compound fence. He saw now why delay had occurred. Once before had he seen the trick used – by eleven SS panzers trapped in a Normandy farmhouse. He had not been officer-in-command on that occasion, had not had to make a decision. As it happened the SS panzers had no hope of escape; Allied forces were swarming all over the area. Here, however, the situation was reversed. The Chinese bandits were not trapped. They were the attackers and had no excuse.

Allison said, 'Oh, my God!'

Indian women, children, and Malay Chinese came shuffling up the pad by the fence driven from behind and within the crowd by the guns of the guerrillas. The CTs were obvious in their jungle greens but it would have been impossible to pick them off buried as they were in the herd of tappers.

Grief and fear congealed into fury in Allison Wingfield.

She shouted, *'Shoot! Shoot!'*

Deacon took position behind the Lewis gun, its rear and fore sights swinging on to the advancing mob.

The woman shouted again, *'Shoot them, Deacon!'*

Hostages: if he hesitated much longer the guerrillas would be within charging distance and the bungalow would be overwhelmed.

Fury welled in Deacon too. He was being forced to play Sand Shan's foul game, to make pawns of the innocent. He tilted the Lewis with his forefinger, aimed the sight above the mob, on the indistinct group a quarter of a mile away, veiled by smoke drift. He had no opportunity to use the binoculars, to ascertain if Shan was among them.

The woman was beside him. He could hear the soft womanly explosions of breath as she squeezed the trigger of the Enfield rifle. She fired straight into the crowd.

Deacon fired too.

The guerrilla leaders scattered at once, diving away. Two

writhed and fell. Perhaps Wei Sand Shan was one of them, though Deacon doubted it. Impulsively he swept the Lewis down and through, scything an arc of high-powered bullets into the phalanx below.

Below and behind, he caught the din of rifle fire. Shan's élite had stormed the garden once more. Buz would have his hands full. But Deacon was caught up in his own fight, one of brutal necessity. He heard the click and flat clatter of the Enfield's empty clip hitting the floor as the woman reloaded, then the bark and long sigh of a mortar shell, a muffled explosion below. A pillar of earth went up, higher than the roof. Dirt rained down on the tiles. Deacon didn't stop firing. Elbows tucked into his sides, chin pointed down the Lewis gun's hot muzzle, he completed his part in the outrage, mercilessly strafing bandits and civilians. The mob did its best to scatter but it was penned in a fenced area, trapped. Even the bloody CTs – and there were more in the crowd than he had at first imagined – could not evade the stream of bullets.

Return fire from ill-positioned angles *thocked* and whined into the sloping roof and against the stout walls of the tower.

On her knees Allison Wingfield went on shooting, not grunting now but crying out when a shot found a living target. Tapper or bandit, it no longer mattered.

Six or eight bandits had come forward out of the mouth of the cage-like avenue, had flung themselves to the ground along the rim of the compound where it hemmed the lawns. They weren't close enough to be under the protection of the roof eaves yet, had no shelter at all. Besides, in the living-room below, P.B. McNair had a crossfire on them and picked off a pair who were foolish enough to try to belly-crawl towards the verandah.

Deacon took out the remaining raiders with four short bursts.

Heaving, tappers and bandits made a quagmire of bodies, some on the wire itself. If it hadn't been for the women and children, it would have been a perfect rat-shoot and Deacon would have been howling in triumph. But he recognised a massacre when he saw it, had a vision of his career as an officer going west.

The impregnability of the tower gave him a false impression of superiority; the devil in a high place pointing the finger of death without discrimination. His mouth tasted of black powder. His ears sang with the stammer of the Lewis gun and screaming from the compound. He hammered off the empty pan with the heels of his hands and locked another into the spindle. He could hardly see for sweat.

He wasn't at all prepared for the mortar shell.

It arched across the roof from north to south and failed to find the tower by less than twenty feet. Shards of red tile, sharp as axe blades, whistled all around. The slump of debris pouring inwards through the roof of the bungalow sounded like a snow avalanche. Peripherally Deacon noticed that Shan's men had set fire to the rubber trees along the north-western edge. Already the choking stench of spluttering resin was thick in the air. Hunched under the corner of the wall, one hand still on the grip of the Lewis gun, Deacon grabbed Allison Wingfield by the waist and yanked her down beside him.

She turned her face like a lover and smiled warmly.

'We've got them on the run. Haven't we? *Damn it, haven't we*?'

'Absolutely,' said Deacon. 'But they've found our range.'

'What?'

'We had best get out of here.'

'*What*?' She was appalled at the notion of retreat.

Perhaps she had imagined that the tower would be her tomb.

Dearly he would have liked to save the Lewis gun but it was an awkward brute and he did not dare tarry, not with the mortar crew there on the jungle's edge, dickering with the range screw and revising the elevations. The next shell would be dropped into the centre of the tower with all the precision of Santa Claus popping down a chimney.

Deacon scrambled back, hoisted open the trap and caught Allison Wingfield by the arm. She struggled, the smile gone. She was battle-crazed, strung out. He got his arms around her and bodily dragged her to the trap, pushed her down without dignity. The Enfield almost took his ear off as she hauled it after her.

Deacon slithered head first over the edge of the trap. He braced himself on the steep stepladder. The woman was sitting on her backside on the parquet floor below, looking up at him in astonishment as if he had commited an impropriety. Deacon pushed himself away from the ladder and on to her and slid her beneath him against the stout wooden posts which cornered the broad central corridor.

With a skull-splintering crack, a mortar shell struck the inner wall of the tower and blew the structure out by the roots.

Dust and flints of concrete hosed down into the corridor and the roof beams groaned loudly. Deacon heard the platform on which the tower had been built break from its piles and go smashing down on to the verandah below.

Allison wriggled softly below him but he did not relent. He pressed on her with his flanks and belly to keep her still. Sure enough, a second shell followed the hitter and the ceiling caved in directly beneath the trap. The wooden ladder folded up and there was wood everywhere plus a zoo of lizards, moths and small drowsy bats, evicted from the space beneath the tiles.

Hoisting himself on to his knees, Deacon dragged the woman – who was still clutching her rifle as if it was a baby – along the corridor and into the office. Clive's office.

She cried, '*I'm all right*! *I'm all right, Damn you, Captain Deacon*', in a peevish quavering voice.

Glass littered the floor of the office. Blast had swirled a blizzard of loose papers everywhere. But the walls and ceiling were intact and the big mahogany desk, the swivel chair and the ant-proof metal filing cabinets were in place. An empty whisky glass stood on the desk where the dead planter had left it late the previous night, along with his leather-bound account books.

All of this Deacon took in at a glance, particularly the open jagged frame of the window to the front. He hardly noticed the window on the side of the bungalow. It was covered with a split-bamboo blind which laid a honey-coloured patch upon the polished floor.

Allison got to her feet. Deacon was already at the shattered window, taking stock of what was happening in the compound. To his gratification he saw that the bandits had pulled back. They were grouping raggedly behind the smoking shacks. Heat whorled the left-hand flank of the compound. Smuts of sooty material floated over the abandoned lawns and inner fence. Though Deacon could not see them, P.B. apparently had reasonable targets in view and the rifle fire was steady, deliberate punctuation in the lull.

From the back kitchen, however, there was no sound. He would have to check on Buz, make sure the sergeant hadn't bought it. Surprisingly, the mortar sent over no more shells.

For half a minute longer the Captain watched the darting figures of the guerrillas as they gave the bungalow a wide berth, drawn by a signal to the left. When Deacon turned, Allison had a glass of whisky in her hand.

She drank, dabbed her lips with her wrist, then fussed with her straggling hair. She was trembling.

'God!' she said. 'I must look an awful mess.'

A brass-cased ship's clock was screwed to the inner wall of the office. It was only twenty minutes past eight. Already the terrorists had demolished their strongest position, the tower on the roof.

Allison said, 'We're not going to be able to hold, are we?'

'Of course we are.'

'Want some?'

She offered the whisky bottle.

Deacon said, 'Why not?'

He took the bottle and tipped a mouthful of the stuff between his dry lips. What he really wanted was tea, about half a gallon of hot sweet tea. He held the spirits in his mouth and let it trickle down his throat then resolutely put down the bottle.

Allison turned to set the empty glass on the desk.

The window on the gable wall exploded inwards. Only the bamboo blind prevented her from being flayed by flying glass.

'*Down*!' Deacon shouted.

He dropped to one knee as the Communists charged the window.

Bullets whirred in the office, carving a path for the raiders.

The bamboo buckled, the first intruder silhouetted against it.

'*Down*, *Allison*!' Deacon yelled again.

He flung the grenade with all his might, not a lob but a straight, fast, side-arm pitch, as he might have hurled a baseball. He was no more than twenty feet from the window but such was the force with which he hurled the object that it carried the fine, rattling bamboo shade with it and dropped outside the frame.

The CT raiding party had been crouched against the side of the house. The grenade tumbled among them and exploded instantly.

It was weirdly like a puppet drama: shadows of tossed bodies against the honey-coloured shade; then the curtain ripped from its rings and flew quite intact across the office like a magic carpet, revealing sunlight stippled with dark dirt.

The guerrilla who had had the misfortune to be half across the windowsill was gutted by the blast. His torso collapsed across the sill. The weapon in his hands projected forward and clattered on the floor only feet from the Captain's hands. The Japanese helmet, lifted off the bandit's skull along with a flap of flesh like a divot of grass, rolled about on the floor too.

Deacon dived for the submachine-gun; a Japanese type 100 first-pattern, immediately identifiable by its clumsy bayonet bar, tangent-leaf rearsight and rough weld seams. The curved side-fitting magazine would hold thirty 8mm cartridges. Deacon prayed to God that it was nearly full. He snapped at the unfamiliar mechanisms, cradled the muzzle on his left hand and advanced, firing in eight- or ten-round bursts into the vaporous hole in the office wall.

If a second unit thrust forward then he was done for. But half-deaf, his vision blurred by smoke, Deacon felt in his belly a rekindled fire, the angry heat of battle stripped of formalities and strategies. Whoever was out there was an enemy. Whoever got in his way must die. He cocked a knee under the chest of the dead bandit and heaved the corpse back over the remains of the sill. He craned and sprayed the area with the submachine-gun as if it was a canister of insecticide.

There had been six of them. They had come close, padding from the rubber and the yellow scrub which lay on the bungalow's right flank. The strike on the tower had been their signal to penetrate the office. Shan had probably briefed the team with a plan of the house, handed out by the servant. Deacon stuck his head out of the hole but saw nothing moving. Shan wasn't so clever after all. He should have backed the raiding team with snipers.

Deacon snapped his head back inside. The mangled blood-spattered remains below the window did not revolt him and the bland untrammelled faces of the Chinese staring up from the dirt roused no whit of pity.

He wheeled round.

The woman was behind the desk, the Enfield trained.

She said, 'Are they all dead?'

'Yes.'

'How many?'

'Six.'

'That's six less. Shall we push the filing cabinets against the window?'

Deacon nodded.

'And the desk?'

'The desk too,' said Deacon. 'But we had better hurry.'

As it happened they had plenty of time to make the room secure.

Wei Sand Shan did not attack again until twenty-five minutes to ten, about which time, unknown to the combatants at the plantation, Gurkha Johnny Badhur and a near-naked Dyak with a human head in a bag on his back, bent over the handlebars of their Raleigh roadsters, were panting down Port Kernan's elegant high street towards the gates of the garrison camp.

'What I can't figure out,' said Buz Campbell through a mouthful of cold rice and chicken, 'is why the little sonuvabitch hasn't tried to burn us out.'

'Aye, what the hell's he waitin' for?' said P.B.

Deacon spooned the last of the savoury rice from the bowl and wiped his mouth fastidiously on a clean linen handkerchief which Allison had found for him. 'He wants to take us alive if he can.'

'What for?' P.B. persisted.

'So that he can execute us in front of the assembled natives,' said Deacon. 'It's one of Shan's less appealing foibles. His style, you might say.'

'Jesus!' Buz murmured.

'But why?' said Allison Wingfield.

'If the indigenous population actually sees the white *tuans* and their lackeys – us, the military – tortured and humiliated, the theory is that they will soon realise where the power in the land really lies.'

'With the Commies,' said Buz.

'Tyranny, in other words,' said Deacon.

It was hardly a *tête-à-tête* conversation. The soldiers were not together during the meal which Allison Wingfield had prepared. They remained behind improvised barricades, Buz to the rear of the bungalow, P.B. and Deacon on watch at the front.

The office had been 'sealed' with filing cabinets and the huge desk, which it had taken all three men to move. Their guns were loaded and laid to hand. Deacon had prowled from room to room to ensure that there were no intruders. By the look of it, Wei Sand Shan too had stopped for a breather and to allow his men to breakfast. There was no sign of activity between the verandah steps and the outer wire at the mouth of the road. Where Shan had imprisoned the native families Deacon did not know. Shan had shown some of the milk of human kindness by sending out a white flag party of six unarmed guerrillas to stretcher away the wounded. He had had the injured civilians taken away too, though God knew what he would do with them.

The scene was one of peaceful devastation.

P.B. had shinned up the shattered steps and eased himself through the hole in the bungalow's roof to make a recce. He had reported that the guerrillas were grouped on the edge of old rubber, a half-mile to the right, beyond the burned-out lines.

Deacon had asked Allison to find food and dry clothing.

Allison had changed into a pale-green shirt and jodhpurs. She had also unearthed more ammunition for the Vaughan, plus two Luger automatics with boxes of 9 mm cartridges, weapons that she had not known were in the house and which came to light in a drawer in Clive's desk.

P.B. had one of the automatics tucked into his belt, Deacon the other.

Everything would have been just dandy, Buz reckoned, if only the woman could have come up with spare parts for the radio. But Clive, she said, had never been 'awfully keen' on the radio and had given it space only because the planters' defence and security committee insisted on it. Anyhow the goddamned set had been screwed up good by the houseboy. It would have taken a signals wizard, not just a jack-of-all-trades like Buz, to fix it and make it function.

Buz said, 'Yeah, the Chink must be goddamned confident to hang off like this, goddamned sure we can't make contact with the town or with patrol units who might be in the neighbourhood.'

'He's confident of his ability to slink back into the jungle,' said Deacon. 'After all, he has made rather a decent score as it is.'

'He's destroyed the Wade-Wingfield,' said Allison matter-of-factly. 'With Clive . . . my . . . my husband gone . . . And so much damage.'

Deacon said, 'He's only burned a few of the rubber trees, Allison. I'm sure the plantation will be viable in a week or two, given a modicum of reinvestment.'

'Who'll buy it now, after a . . . a massacre?'

Buz said, 'Somebody'll take it off your hands, ma'am. If there's money to be made, bandits won't stop investors.'

Deacon said, 'There may not be any bandits in the area by then. It's Sand Shan's territory, his exclusive domain, and Wei Sand Shan can't escape the security net for ever.'

Buz said, 'Yeah, maybe not. But we sure as hell ain't gonna get him today, Deke.'

'Oh, you never know,' said Deacon.

'Not unless one of the other units, "Tracy" or "Flynn", comes rollin' over the ridge, and that ain't very liable.'

'No,' said Deacon. 'The best we can hope for in that direction is the arrival of "A" Squadron from Port Kernan.'

'What if Shan's gotten an ambush ready?' said Buz.

'I'm sure he will have,' said Deacon. 'But our chaps won't

charge blindly up the road. They'll be extremely circumspect, unless I miss my guess.'

They finished the meal and drank down the last of the big pot of tea which the woman had brewed in the kitchen.

Breakfast over, the SAS men returned to their vigils.

Outside, the morning was alive with the drone of insect colonies feeding on the corpses. There were bush rats too, tempted out in numbers by the odour of blood. A pair of dingy brown vultures, rare in that part of the state, had got wind of the carrion and were crabbing furtively along the sagging top of the wire, intent on a bloody object which lay against it. Out back, between the kitchen and the store barns, there was no movement at all apart from pecking chickens and the nervous dart of swallows from the shadow of the huts.

P.B. watched the vultures. He would have put a bullet through each of the filthy creatures if he'd had leisure and ammo to spare. Deacon had told him, long before in the desert, that scavengers were an essential part of the natural cycle. P.B. understood the lesson but he could not abide the bloody slinking things with their wicked beaks, beady eyes and ugly agile necks. He tried not to watch the birds as they parachuted down from the wire and began feeding on a corpse.

The sunlit air was tainted by the stench of decay and the acrid tang of the smouldering trees and half-fired smokehouse.

For forty minutes there was no sound from the guerrillas, only an occasional glimpse of figures flitting through the young rubber. Waiting was wearing on the nerves. Behind the sofa in front of the smashed glass of the living-room window P.B. smoked cigarette after cigarette, grew more and more tensely alert, until each corpulent flutter of the vultures' wings, each scuttle of a rat, made his eyes blink and his normally steady hand tremble.

'Come on, y'bastards, come on, come on,' he murmured beneath his breath.

Common sense told him that the longer the bandits held off, the more chance there was of the Dyak and the Gurkha reaching a radio and summoning help. None of them doubted that Johnny Badhur and Umgah had made good their escape. Even so, there was still the niggling suspicion that the CTs might have caught and executed them.

Though he had been through a physical ordeal, an all-night trek plus a dawn battle, P.B. was wide awake. There would be time for sleep later; a dram from Wingfield's whisky bottle and a long, long rest. He had already earned the right to fight again, had made his bones with the new SAS. The Deke wouldn't chuck him out of the squadron now, no matter what happened.

Corporal McNair lit another cigarette. Three more ugly wattle-necked birds winged clumsily down from the tops of the rubber trees and sidled along the ground.

P.B. decided not to watch them feed.

He glanced at his wrist-watch.

It was 09.22 hours.

The vultures heard it first. The unfamiliar noise distracted them from their feeding.

P.B. heard it too. He couldn't make it out either.

He shouted, 'Jeff, what the bloody hell's yon?'

'I . . . I'm not sure.'

Buz came through from the rear of the bungalow, his head cocked and a puzzled expression on his face. He stooped by the side of the sofa and screwing up his eyes squinted into the sky.

'Goddamned funny!' he said.

Gobbling, beating their wings hard, the five vultures abandoned the meat and took to the air.

From his position by the doorway Deacon shouted, 'It's a helicopter! I didn't know there were any on this side of the border.'

'A helicopter!' Buz shouted. 'Hey, ain't that keen, man? They've sent a helibird to rescue us!'

The helicopter appeared over the trees above the Port Kernan road. It seemed to ride the air as softly as a dragonfly. The skin of its bulbous body shone in the sunlight while its three-bladed main rotor glistened and its little tail rotor whisked like an egg-switch.

Buz cheered and punched the air.

Imperiously Deacon shouted, '*Keep down*! *Nobody move*!'

'Yeah! Yeah! Okay! Okay!'

And P.B. said, 'It is nae one of ours, Buz.'

'Jesus!' Buz Campbell said. 'It's a Ruskie!'

Carefully P.B. dropped his cigarette to the floor. He licked his thumb and ground out the coal with it. He licked his thumb again and, calmly now, settled the rifle butt to his shoulder.

But the helicopter, later identified as a Mi-1 Hare, dropped down out of sight to the east, and for five more minutes the Scot had nothing to shoot at.

'A helibird! Jesus! What the fuck are these jungle rats doin' with a 'copter?' Buz bawled indignantly. 'The British goddamned Army don't have anything like that. What the fuck are they doin', Deke?'

'Flying in ammunition,' Deacon answered.

'Uh-oh!' Buz shouted from the rear of the house.

'What?'

'I got me a mortar crew back here,' Buz announced.

'That's what I was afraid of,' Deacon said.

One minute later the final bombardment began.

Deacon to Holms: August 1951

It was the first indication any of us had – by which I mean Malayan Military Intelligence – that the guerrillas had stolen a march on us by purchasing a general utility air machine. It was not a model which I had ever seen before, but Campbell's guess that it was Russian in origin was spot on. Mud had been daubed over the underbelly markings but, as it hovered over the road, I could just discern them, and they were Russian.

All sorts of thoughts chased through my mind, spiced, as you may imagine, by outraged anger at the notion of Wei Sand Shan having wings at his disposal. Naturally I didn't have much opportunity to speculate on how the CT leader had acquired the helicopter or what sort of organisation was required to service it. It was obvious that it had been summoned by radio from a secret base in the hills and had brought in a quantity of ammunition including mortar shells.

The delay had been occasioned by the wait for the Hare. Shan, however, was too sound a general to waste precious time. He had set up the mortars in strategic positions, out of sight of the house windows in the cover of the young rubber. He had also repositioned his assault teams. He planned to use flank fire from the mortars as cover for a four-pronged attack upon the house. No hit-and-run methods for my Chinese opponent. He seemed to be saying that if the British wanted a *real* war he would be only too happy to oblige.

It was difficult to estimate how many guerrillas were left under arms. At a rough guess I would have put the number at about one hundred and fifty; but it may have been less. The helicopter was far too small, of course, to ferry in troops. Besides, I seriously doubted if Shan had manpower reserves in the state.

I had built a fox-hole of sorts by the front door of the bungalow. The door itself I had removed from its hinges and placed laterally across six sandbags which Buz and P.B. had manhandled down from the roof. There wasn't much heavy furniture in the bungalow, apart from the office, but Allison had found two teak-wood blanket-chests which I had wedged against the posts with timber scrounged from the smashed stepladder. Really it was a reasonable sort of 'stand' and would have held against bullets and even grenades. But against a direct hit from a 2 lb mortar shell it would be totally ineffectual.

The whistle of the first shells was terrifying.

Gouts of earth were torn up all along the front of the house, a solid curtain of dark brown and red, out of which at any second I expected Shan's grenadiers to appear. It did not take me long to cotton on to the fact that the guerrillas did not intend to blitz the bungalow. Shan was determined to take us alive.

I didn't flatter myself that he knew it was me.

There was no gladiatorial nonsense about it, however. I was no more a thorn in Shan's flesh than a dozen other trackers and sniffers who wanted his head on their wall. He had no clue that I was in the Wingfield. Chinese guerrillas are not as a rule prone to hunches.

I had decided to let the gable walls of the bungalow take care of themselves. Allison was crumbling under the fusilade and begged me not to send her into some far part of the house on her own. I told her to stay with me. She perked up a little and got herself on her knees with the Enfield balanced across the edge of the door. She turned her head, I remember, and struggled to smile. I winked. It was very heroic, the more so because it seemed that we were doomed.

Logic informed me that a rescue party would not arrive from Port Kernan much before 13.00 hours at the earliest. 'Tracy' and 'Flynn', unless they had seriously lost their way, were separated from the Wade-Wingfield by several densely forested ridges and I did not imagine that the Hare would have flown over them or, if it had, that it would have drawn them magnetically to the plantation. Stupid, how one clutches at straws: it would have taken either unit a day of hard slog to reach us. But all sorts of ridiculous notions pranced about in my brain as I waited for the frontal assault group to show itself during the signalled lull in mortar shelling.

I had already decided that it would be madness to retreat to the cellar beneath the house. There we would be trapped completely and would have no opportunity to 'dig out'. In darkness, perhaps. By daylight, futile. Part of my reluctance to retreat into a corner stemmed from my training. There is something unholy to an officer of Special Air Service about dying in a hole.

I had already made up my mind that if the verandah to the front of the house was breached I would endeavour to lead a break-out through the kitchen and try to reach the jungle to the rear. Our chances of lying low, even if we did make it across the open ground, were slender but at least we would die fighting which was a damned better prospect than being taken alive. There was always a chance, faint though it was, that accident might bring Sand Shan and me together face to face.

Impatiently I waited for the smoke to clear.

P.B. shouted, '*See them! Left. Left. T'the bloody left!*'

The Chinese were running fast and upright, Jap weapons held at the port, a dozen of them were aiming for the gable. P.B. had a poor field of fire. In half a minute the group would establish itself under the bungalow wall. Shelling ceased while the infantry advanced.

Buz shouted, 'I got twenty back here!'

I vaulted over the barricade and flung myself on to the verandah. Smoke clung to the fabric of the house. I counted on a few seconds' advantage. I pitched both grenades one after another, turned and shouted to Allison to toss me the Sten.

She was already on her feet. The weapon came at me straight and hard. I grabbed it, swivelled and fired a continuous burst. Still firing, I ran along the verandah. I could see very little. I had no idea whether or not I was finding targets. When I reached the living-room window, I kicked splintered glass from the bottom of the frame and stepped inside.

'Grand day,' said P.B. by way of greeting.

The corporal continued firing while I hurried through the house to the kitchen to see how Buz was faring.

The mortar there had holed the chain-link. The bandits were trying again. They had divided into three groups. Two gave heavy covering fire to the vanguard. Buz was doing sterling work in delaying them. But there was simply too many for a solo gunner to cope with.

The kitchen was a mess. Pans and other utensils had been shot from their hooks. The panelled walls were gouged with bullet holes. The fly-screen door, hanging on its hinges, had practically been demolished by shot. The narrow verandah was strewn with debris. My notion of making an escape via the kitchen yard seemed silly. There and then I began to consider alternatives. By sheer weight of numbers we would be overwhelmed if we stayed where we were.

'Hold as long as you can, Buz.'

'Will do, Deke.'

He had given up random fire and was taking his time, making every shot count.

I backed out of the kitchen and through the long corridor to the office. I opened the door and flattened myself against it. All was quiet within. Apparently Shan had given up on that wing. I clambered on to the big desk and cautiously hoisted the remains of the bamboo blind. There wasn't a sign of a Communist. It was peaceful, incredibly peaceful.Four small red bantams pecked the dirt only yards from me. The rubber's grey-green frieze against the enormous trees of the jungle seemed so close that I felt I could step into it straight from the window ledge.

I looked out. The stink of the corpses under the window enveloped me like a gas. I held my breath.

Beyond the gable's end I could make out the helicopter, a long way off, at the big swing of the compound on the Port Kernan road. Men were clustered by the 'copter, a dozen or so. They appeared to be uninterested in the attack. It seemed that Wei Sand Shan was not the type of leader who cared to risk his neck in close combat. I could not, of course, identify Shan at that distance. But I knew he would be there, directing infantry units and mortar crews like a chess master.

I was puzzled by the fact that I could not see the mortar. It should have been in sight somewhere along the tree-line. The implacable trees might be infested with bandits for all I could tell: waiting rifles; patient and inscrutable, under orders to hang fire. It would not be above Shan's deductive ability to reason that we would look for an exit, to cunningly offer us one.

'*Jeffrey. Jeffrey. Quickly!*'

I had almost forgotten Mrs Wingfield. Her urgent cry brought me back from the office into the central corridor again.

She was stretched across the door frame not, as I at first imagined, wounded but to obtain a better angle for the Enfield.

Guerrillas were stealing up through the tappers' lines, a great heart-stopping swarm of them. The mortar crew were in the front rank carrying the little weapon. The advance was disciplined. Blackened timbers gave the bandits protection, particularly as we had no great weight of fire to pin them down. We could not hold out against a concentrated attack.

I pulled Allison inside. I discharged an entire magazine from the Sten in the general direction of the lines, though I knew it would be of little benefit. I pushed the woman down the corridor and cried for Buz and P.B. to fall back. There was no choice but to make a break through the window of Wingfield's office, try to reach the shelter of the trees.

Without Allison we might have been able to out-run the bandits and would certainly have dispersed the moment we struck cover. But she would not be fit enough to tackle an all-out dash through the brush. She clung to me, as if suspecting that I might abandon her. Buz leapt from the kitchen, slamming the door behind him.

I pointed. 'In there. Wait!'

P. B. McNair came next. He had an unopened whisky bottle in his left hand, a Sten in his right and the Luger tucked handily into his belt. He had lost his beret and his hair stuck up in comical tufts.

'There.'

'Right.'

I disentangled myself from Allison and extracted my last two grenades. I tweaked out the pins and held the levers, a grenade in each hand.

The doorway was rimed with sunlight and shooting started again when the phalanx of the CTs reached the end of the tappers' lines and spread along the remains of the wire. I did not dare show myself. I rolled the grenades over the barricade and let them bounce down the verandah steps. Swiftly I stepped after Allison into the office.

The metal filing-cabinets which defended the window to the front of the house rattled with the blast from the grenades. The brass clock dropped off the wall.

Hell broke loose.

Mortar shells crumped into the bungalow front and rear. Lead flew everywhere. The bandits shouted as they rushed the verandah, or what was left of it. I realised that we had come very close to the point of no return.

'Out!' I snapped.

P.B. did not question my command or demand to know if I had checked the situation beyond the small window. He climbed nimbly up on to the top of the desk and, still carrying his damned whisky bottle, glanced back.

'Where to, Deke?'

'A beeline for the rubber.'

'Right. See you.'

P.B. raised the bottle, pulled up the frayed end of the bamboo and stepped down among the dead Communists. Smoke like ectoplasm drifted in the sunlight.

P.B. stuck his head back into the room. 'It's okay. Bring on the lady.'

I could hardly believe it.

Allison went next, Buz following. I came last.

I wished I'd had the foresight to dig up another grenade. The firing had reached such a pitch of intensity, however, that one grenade would hardly have had much effect, even as a diversion. God knew where Shan had acquired such quantities of ammunition. The Wingfield bungalow received thousands of rounds in the space of three or four minutes. If the guerrillas had been a mite less forceful, they might have noticed the absence of return fire and have twigged what we were up to. The north-west gable of the Wingfield bungalow with its blown window had, however, been neglected.

The trees which had seemed so marvellously close from the shelter of four walls now appeared miles away. The distance in fact was a couple of hundred yards. Two little outbuildings, like rural water-closets, stuck up in solitary splendour in the side section. The bantams had gone squawking off and a startled flock of something-or-others wheeled against the sky above the jungle foliage. The silent stand of rubber, scrubbed clean of underbrush, was menacing. P.B. was already sprinting towards it. He knew that his job was to provide some kind of covering fire.

I bawled at Buz to clear out but he would not leave us. Indeed, if Campbell *had* gone I would not be writing to you now.

Buz provided back-cover while I grabbed Mrs Wingfield and ran with her towards the trees. There would come a moment when the gable would no longer screen us and we would be in full view of the bandits. But before that moment arrived a four-man advance party appeared round the wall from the verandah. All carried rifles, not submachine-guns. They were shocked to stumble on us and recovered too late.

Buz Campbell mowed them down. They screamed like tortured animals, ringing shrieks which immediately drew other guerrillas to the place.

Buz shouted, '*Get going, Deke, for Chrissake*!'

On his belly in the dirt, still short of the trees by thirty yards, P.B. furnished us with covering fire. The whisky bottle stood up beside him, golden in the sun, like a portable headstone.

I practically lifted Allison from her feet and swept on with her past P.B. I had seldom felt so exposed. Hordes of terrorists had been diverted from the main thrusts on the house and were streaming towards us now. I remember thinking that this was how a fox must feel in a bare November field when the hounds are in full tongue and the covert is too far off to reach.

Allison fell, pitching headlong. My arm was almost jerked from its socket. The fall knocked all breath from her. Though bullets were thick in the air, oddly it did not occur to me that she had been hit.

I knelt by her side, drawing out the Luger.

Buz had backed as far as the scrape where P.B. was lying and the pair braced themselves as Communists fanned across the curve of the lawn, below its protective breast. From the back of the bungalow Shan's men were congregating too. Some bright sparks among them would surely steal into the rubber to cut off our line of retreat. There was no hope now. Allison was incapable of running. Besides, if we raised ourselves we would surely be cut to pieces. There were just too damned many of them.

Allison drew the little pistol from the holster at her waist and held it in both hands.

Buz and P.B. were pinned down in a shallow scrape on the broad track where trucks reversed up to the smokehouse. It seemed that we were not destined to escape after all.

'Look!' Allison said.

She had rolled on to her elbow, face turned to the sky. She was wounded, bush shirt stained with blood but paid no heed to her injury. She pointed with the pistol. The helicopter hovered fifty feet above the ground then, as we watched, began an awkward swooping troll across the open space.

'*Shit*!' Buz shouted. '*Bombs*!'

Explosions – a fusillade of small-arms fire – confusion – groups of terrorists gaping, pointing as if they had never seen Shan's command 'copter before. The machine dumped down on the crown of the lawn. Settling heavily on tricycle landing gear, its tail boom whirled grass dust in a fierce tornado.

The four jeeps and four ten-tonners were big, fresh-looking jobs. The Port Kernan Security Police kept its transport as spick and span as fire-engines. Behind them were two more trucks which I identified as the ones Tim Dalinart had requisitioned for SAS use in the interim period of establishment. The SAS vehicles had already disgorged half their complement of soldiers. The lads advanced in a beautifully solid line behind the trucks. How Johnny Badhur had got word to the town in such a short space of time was more than I could fathom. But there they were, an eager force of British and Malay fighting men, all properly armed.

Buz had seen too many soldiers whipped by stray bullets in the dying minutes of battle to stand up and do his war-dance. He kept well down. I could see his Sten waving in delight, however.

The helicopter lifted, hopped over the roof of the bungalow and dumped down on uneven ground between the house and the store barns. It appeared to be picking up troops. But the Hare was a three-man machine and I was puzzled by what it was doing there. Then it dawned on me. I had been quite wrong in my assessment of Wei Sand Shan. The little bugger hadn't been 'down the road' at all. He'd been steering the assault from the rear. The 'copter pilot was seeking Shan, to whisk him away to safety.

The firing had swung round, like a wind. Communists were putting up little resistance. They knew they had been caught fair and square and had no hope of defeating the security forces which, like trawl nets, were sweeping across the area. Any resistance that the terrorists put up was merely to delay our advance.

'Are you badly injured, Allison?' I asked.

'No,' she answered. 'No, I don't think so.'

'You're safe enough here. But lie low, please.'

'Jeff, where . . .?'

'I've a little bit of unfinished business to attend to.'

Bandits were running south and south-east into the deep jungle which lay close to the spur of the plantation. Some had gone back up the trail. Other groups were sprinting along the jeep track which meandered through the upper sections. I could leave pursuit and mopping-up to police trackers and our chaps from 'A' Squadron. There would be plenty of wounded bandits to interrogate and corpses to yield secrets from their pockets. It would be a long hot day for coppers and soldiers.

It's amazing how easily one accepts salvation. The aftermath of action, that smothering weariness marked by disgust and despair, had not come upon me yet. I had my eye on the helicopter.

I broke north into the skirts of young rubber. Charred, blistered and reeking, the smokehouse gave me a long screen. I went behind it and running fast cleared it and veered right.

The fact that he was hatless and wore a pair of gold-rimmed spectacles put me on to Sand Shan. He still had that wand-slender neck and alert carriage of the head, still resembled a schoolboy. He did not look in the least like the leader of a gang of ruthless guerrillas. He bore no visible arms. He sported a pale-green nylon shirt and lightweight ducks and was as obvious as a London bus there in the scrubble of the battlefield.

Two hefty Chinks in battledress were solicitiously escorting him towards the helicopter as if he were a visiting diplomat. They were ducked forward, leaning into the writhing wind of the rotor blades. A dozen or so bandits were hopping and leaping like kangaroo rats towards the barns and shelter beyond. None hung back to give Wei Sand Shan cover. The Russian Hare looked huge in the enclosed space, cumbersome too. It had barely touched down when it lifted and bumped, twirled and bumped again with reckless impatience.

One damned grenade would have done for it. A stream of Sten-gun bullets into the fuselage or through the flickering blades and I would have had him. But I had no grenades and no weapon except Clive Wingfield's old Luger. To be frank, the sight of Shan there before me was enough to sweep away all caution, all sense. I had a sudden vision of Shan escaping, rising on silver wings like a dragon, away over the jungle. I went just a little mad, I suppose.

Weaving, I ran towards the craft. The pilot must have caught sight of me and panicked. He lifted off, leaving Shan and his bodyguards flattened by down-draught and half-blinded by dust. They shouted up at the hovering 'copter and it dropped solidly and seemed to bounce. One of the bodyguards picked Shan up by the waist and bundled him into the craft through the narrow side door.

Full payload, as it turned out, was one pilot and three troops. The Ivchenko engine could not efficiently cope with more. I was thirty yards from the Hare. The bodyguards still hadn't spotted me. They were too concerned with hoisting themselves into the aircraft. Through the smeared glass of the cabin window I could just make out the pilot; Shan too. The 'copter strained and rose. One bodyguard hung from it by his arm.

I pumped five shots from the Luger.

The bandit fell to the ground. His comrade pivoted. I shot him too. The Hare thudded down then rose away from the slope in a great swerving glide only six or eight feet off the dirt, like a huge sword blade intended to slice me in half.

If I had dropped, Shan would have had me. But I was transfixed. I didn't flinch as the daubed metal belly swept past me. Instead, I snatched at the struts of the landing gear and was whisked into the air.

The climb rate of rotor-wing aircraft is in the order of fifteen feet per second. We were no higher than that when my fingers found the edge of the slam door. I muscled my chest and belly over the lip and heaved myself inside.

Dazed, breathless, I rolled away from the door as the Hare suddenly soared and tilted. I had a blurred glimpse of rubber then boiling green jungle foliage, an image curved like a buckled postcard. I pitched violently against the wall of the fuselage. I fought to regain balance. Shan's face was a pale blob against the windows of the cab.

I think Shan was shouting. Certainly his mouth was open. He resembled some near-featureless baby. I could not make out the words that Shan shouted. Nothing came through the hive-noise below the rotors. Nothing solidified before my eyes except a liquid sky smitten by dazzles of sunlight, and Wei Sand Shan's head.

From a sprawled position upon the floor, I pumped my last two shots up at that target at a range of less than ten feet.

And I missed.

The bullets *spanged* against the windscreen, powdering the inner surfaces and causing me, in reflex, to duck. The Hare seemed to nod. The guttural roar of the Ivchenko engine flooded the cab, funnelled by wind from the open door. I had no idea what had happened. I assumed that I had killed Sand Shan. But then he was there, scrambling across the body of the Chinese pilot which blocked the controls. The Hare was skimming and slithering all over the sky.

I knew nothing about helicopters but the fragility of the thing was manifest. I had the notion that I was cooked. I grasped the tubular frame of the passenger seat and hauled myself up the incline. It was like a dream again, or a nightmare, for the craft was nose down; yet I had to pull myself with all my strength up the cabin.

Tufted jungle streamed three or four hundred feet below. The craft was travelling north-east. There was no sign of the Wade-Wingfield, the comforting regularity of its rubber plantations had vanished. I had no means of judging air-speed, but we seemed to be travelling with astonishing rapidity.

Wei Sand Shan could not free the controls. He hunched before me, thin-shouldered, his wand-like neck stuck out. I swung with the empty Luger. The 'copter lurched. The Chinese leader grinned at me. My arm came down on the back of the pilot's seat. I knew by the fierce stab of pain that I had broken my wrist. I backhanded with my left arm. A little knife was in Shan's hand. Thin as a needle, but bladed, it ripped the sleeve of my shirt and bared my flesh to the bone. Shan drove the knife at my eyes. I reeled backwards.

That, sir, was the end of our combat.

Even face to face, I'm not at all sure that Shan recognised me.

Oh, he probably did. But he gave no hint of it. I was just

another white man, another imperialist warmonger. The impersonality of it was disheartening. I craved for recognition, not out of vanity but out of an old soldier's need to stamp justice on my cause. All nonsense, under the circumstances.

The Hare was totally out of control. I'm told it should have gone into a spin which would have snapped the rotor blades and plunged it straight into the trees. But helicopters, like people, are not predictable. The Hare wandered on while I clawed at the tubular rigging and tried to find enough stability to get back at Shan.

I didn't even see the trees until they painted out sunlight in the narrow door. Later examination indicated that we had cleared the palms and soft-wood trees by approximately ten feet. We splashed sideways into the waters of Tomah, a lake-swamp of no great area and fortunately of no great depth.

The helicopter came in like a dragonfly. It struck with tailboom first and turned over into thick, receptive waters. I saw daylight and water mix in the curve of the doorway. Rattled about like a cork in a whistle, I groped and thrust myself up out of the craft even as it gurgled and began to sink.

I was bleeding badly and my right arm was numb. I thrust down into the soup, found no bottom and kicked myself on to my back. As you may imagine, I was by now too bruised and beaten to do anything but stroke towards the shore.

Shan was still trapped inside the Hare. I paddled on my back, the helicopter framed between my knees, to make sure that he did not emerge from the mud like a hatched mosquito. Nothing. No Shan. No ripple. Only the abdominal gurgle of the 'copter filling up with sludge. He was gone. Drowned. It was over. Justice done. Debt wiped out. Victory won.

I crawled on to the bank and without taking my eyes off the foundered 'copter lay on my side, leaking blood.

After a time, minutes probably, I drifted into a state of semi-consciousness and was still there, on my side, when the search party finally found me three and a half hours later.

As the crow flies Tomah Lake is nine miles from the edge of the Wade-Wingfield. I was fortunate to have been found at all.

It wasn't our chaps who stumbled on me but a platoon of Malayan Police. With customary efficiency they improvised a stretcher and lugged me back to the highway in spite of my protests that I was – just – fit to walk.

Two or three hours after sunset I was trundled into the tiled interior of the St Andrew's Hospital and given the works. My arm was cleansed and stitched, my wrist set and plastered, my sundry abrasions salved. My questions about the day's 'exercise' at the Wade-Wingfield and the subsequent body count were pointedly ignored, even by the grizzled Scottish doctor, McNeill, who administered a variety of shots to guard against infection. Brusquely McNeill informed me that the hospital and its Roman Catholic annexe in Harbour Head Street were packed with soldiers and civilians in far worse shape than I was, though in my single room on the cool upper floor I saw little activity.

McNeill assured me that my presence as a patient would be notified to the military authority, and had two severe, female, Malay nursing aides tuck me up in bed.

I slept for fifteen hours.

Deacon was standing by the window looking out over the harbour when Major Tim Dalinart entered the room. Deacon wore a washed-out dressing-gown which the staff had found for him. A bowl of soft fruit and a tray of juices stood on the bedside table. The room was tiny and contained only the bed. This did not surprise the Major, for it was on Dalinart's express instruction that the Captain had been granted the privilege of a private ward; at Dalinart's suggestion that the Captain had been detained.

Deacon was awkwardly smoking a cigarette. He transferred it from the fingers of his bandaged hand to the fingers which protruded from the plaster cuff which held the bones of his right wrist in place.

Hearing the door open, Deacon turned.

'About damned time!' he snapped.

'How are you, Jeffrey? Must say you look a trifle the worse for wear.'

'I'm absolutely fine. When do I get out of here?'

'As soon as McNeill's satisfied you've no infection.'

'How long will that be?'

'Two or three days.'

'Good God, Tim! I'm not crocked, you know.'

'Well, you can't handle weapons, can you? I'd say you'd have trouble handling your eating-irons at the moment.'

'Even so . . .' Deacon waved the plastered wrist.

'Aren't you comfortable here?'

'No, damn it!'

'Never mind, old chap. Be out of here in a couple of days, I promise . . .'

'Thank God!'

'. . . on your way to Ceylon.'

'*Ceylon?*'

'Hm!' Dalinart removed the butt of the cigarette from Deacon's fingers and stubbed it out in an ashtray. 'For, let's say, three weeks. Leave. Sick leave. You deserve it.'

'Why Ceylon? Why not Singapore – or home? England.'

'I've a cousin in Kandy. Name's Nigel. Nice chap. He'll look after you. Feed you up, help put you back on your feet.'

'Tim, I'm *on* my feet. I don't need nursing.'

'Worth seeing, Ceylon. Beautiful country.'

'What's wrong, Tim? What's happened? Why are you whisking me away?'

Dalinart seated himself on the bed.

'Might be a tiny bit of trouble with the high brass, old chap. I prefer to keep you out of it.'

'I don't understand. We did the job, didn't we? The squadron didn't disgrace itself, surely. What about "Flynn" and "Tracy"? Don't tell me they—'

'They straggled in this morning. Touch of wobbly tummy here and there, a few cases of heat prostration. Chaps not used to the humidity. No real casualties, though. Didn't meet any bandits. Weren't any. All the bandits were at the Wingfield picnic.'

'Out with it,' said Deacon.

'The mission was incredibly successful. The body count resembles a cricket score. Your little band accounted for fifty-seven dead guerrillas. One hundred-and-seven more were wounded, and over sixty prisoners were taken. Security have had to build a special post-haste stockade for them.'

'How many did we lose?'

'Two dead, seven wounded.'

'Who?'

' "A" Squadron other-ranks. You aren't liable to know them.'

'Why, then, am I in disgrace?'

'One of the Chinkies, one of the bandits, claims you opened fire on a group of workers.'

'That isn't . . . exactly . . . accurate.'

'Oh, no. Dear me, no. I know what happened. Sergeant Campbell and Mrs Wingfield gave accounts in your favour. No choice, had you?'

'No choice at all,' said Deacon.

'Mrs Wingfield claims *she* fired the Lewis gun into the crowd. Is that true?'

Deacon said. 'I can't remember.'

'The problem is our brand-new Commanding Officer. Major Beasely. Fresh out from England. Bit of a mystery man.'

'I thought you were to be Officer Commanding, Tim.'

'Apparently not. Not enough seniority, or some damned thing. Beasely's top dog in Port Kernan. And he isn't at all happy with . . . certain things. Like Dyaks on bicycles with human heads in their luggage.'

'Bicycles? Is that how Johnny and Umgah got to Port Kernan so quickly?'

'Oh, that's a trifle,' said Dalinart. 'The mass slaughter's quite another matter.'

'But we're soldiers, Tim. Listen, my report will explain—'

'No, Jeffrey. No report. No statements or appearances before boards. Not this time. I'm not absolutely positive but I have the feeling that Major Beasely doesn't understand the true nature of the war here.'

Deacon's face was masked by a hard expression which hid his anger well.

'Is Beasely here to disband "K" Squadron?

'It won't come to that.'

'Good God! What do they *want* from us, Tim? I got Shan, didn't I? Wasn't that the whole object – to search out and destroy Wei Sand Shan?'

'You certainly made a very large dent in his army, Jeffrey. Nobody can deny it.'

'And I got Shan.'

'Well, no. Apparently you didn't.'

'*What*?'

'I sent a team of frogmen up to the lake, to Tomah. Not a sign of Shan, dead or alive. We found the pilot. Shot. But no *corpus* for the butcher-boy himself.'

'He was in the helicopter when it went down. I'll swear he was. In the cabin.'

'The frogmen dragged the area. We even winched the wreckage on shore and examined it. Jeffrey, I'm sorry. From all the evidence, it would appear that Wei Sand Shan cannot be listed among the dead.'

'Dear God!'

'So, you see, I need you back here. Not just to chase after Sand Shan. Oh, dear me, no. Shan isn't the only bloody terrorist on the prowl.'

'Dear God!'

'I'd prefer to have you far away in Ceylon while I straighten things out. The *Straits Times* wants to make you a hero. There's a crying need for heroes. But old Beasely—'

'I've got the message, Tim.'

'You go, you come back. All right?'

'All right.'

Dalinart got to his feet. 'I'll send a clerk round with travel warrants and the rest of the bumph tomorrow. You'll like my cousin. Besides, he has two rather nubile daughters who ought to be at home this time of year.'

'Wait,' said Deacon. 'How's Allison Wingfield?'

'Happy to be alive. And grateful to you.'

'Not wounded?'

'Nicked by a bullet on the . . . the chest, shall we say. Won't even be a scar, I'm told.'

Deacon nodded. He had been thinking a lot about Allison Wingfield during the monotonous hours of the afternoon. Wondering what would become of her and if he would ever see her again. But that pleasant, idle line of thought had been driven out by Dalinart's visit and the infuriating news that Wei Sand Shan had escaped.

'Must hasten away, Jeffrey. Sorry,' Tim Dalinart said. 'Don't like to leave the Beezer to his own devices for too long, you know.'

'Of course.'

'Enjoy your leave.'

'Yes.'

'Oh, by the way . . .' The Major hesitated by the door and fumbled in the front of his tunic. 'I have a present for you. Smuggled it past the nurses. It's from McNair. He seemed to think you'll need it.'

Dalinart put the whisky bottle on the table; the same whisky bottle P.B. had rescued from the Wingfield bungalow and had carried through the last action.

Deacon snorted ruefully.

When Dalinart had gone, he opened the slatted window of the hospital room as wide as it would go and looked out across the dark harbour. It was still now, peaceful in that quarter of Port Kernan at this early hour of the evening.

Deacon lay on the top of the bed.

He looked at the whisky bottle. What strength of will McNair must have exercised to keep it capped and intact.

It sat there, golden in the light of the lamp, like a little portable gravestone; then Deacon broke it open and set about getting drunk before the sweet-faced martinets in starched white uniforms could discover him and try to make him behave like a gentleman.